12 Rounds

Fighting Two Rounds at a Time ain't Fair When You Have 12 Rounds to Go

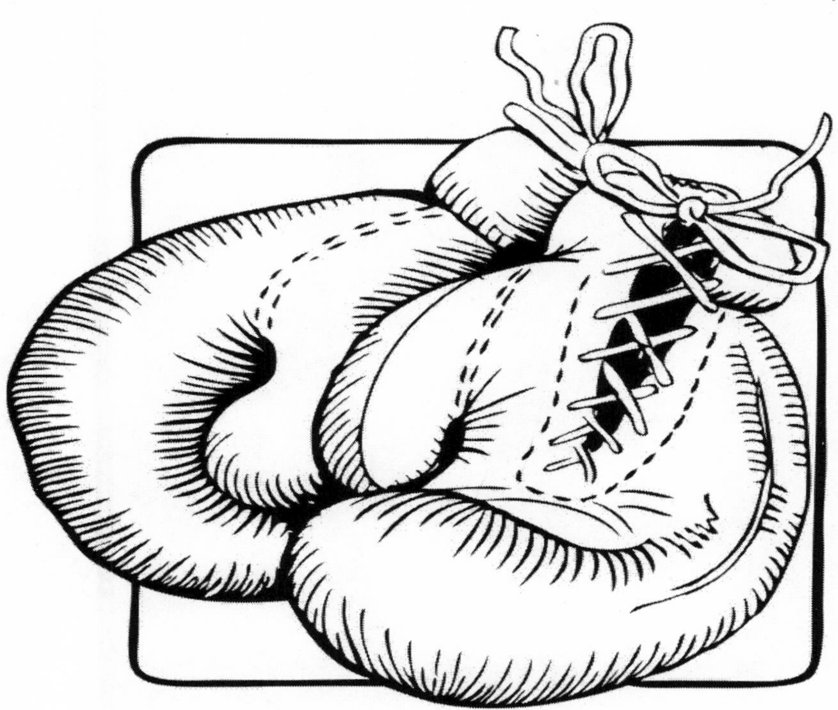

By Octavia Adams

ISBN-13: 978-0578649399

Dedication

This book is dedicated to Dutch, the Broad Street Bullies, Delsea Garden Posse (DGP), the hood of Millville, NJ, and my family.

Table of Contents

Round 1

Punched Drunk

Ky'Nasia entered the ring with the intention of finishing the fight victoriously. She was 5'1" and weighed one hundred and twenty-six pounds, soaking wet. Her eyes were shaped like almonds; she had chestnut brown pupils that were surrounded by a darker brown. Her hair was shoulder length and pressed to the gods. She kept it in a wrap. As a high school freshman, her body was curvy for her age. She had a flat stomach and wore a size five jeans. Her C cup breasts sat pretty in a bra and even better without one, and her body hit all the right measurements. She had it going on, or so she thought.

While attending church, Ky'Nasia met a guy named RahKe. How ironic! The church was where 'Nasia met the devil himself, in disguise of course. RahKe was 5'6" with an athlete's body and had a smile that was to die for. He would flash his grin in every girl's direction, and it would melt their hearts. He thought he was the shit, and 'Nasia couldn't stand him, but his swag and his smile pulled her in. She didn't care for his appearance, but his grin could and did melt her panties right down to the floor. Man, she should have stayed away from that grin.

ht began, Ky'Nasia paced herself, trying to ›r, but the gap between them got bigger. It put he middle of their relationship. On top of the other city, there was an age difference. Plus, nim on the weekends when they both didn't hool sports. After what seemed like forever of not seeing him in church, 'Nasia's god-sister, Tamia invited her to go to his football game. She went to the game with no intention of hooking up with RahKe or anyone else for that matter. She was there to hang out with her sister, but before the game was over, some dude came over and tried to kick it with her. He continued talking to her and followed her around for the rest of the game. When the game ended, RahKe ran over to the car to talk to the fellas. He watched her out of the corner of his eye, then reached over to grab the piece of paper with dude's number on it.

"You won't be needing this. You're here to see me, right?" As he shot his grin her way, he balled up the number and threw it in the air. They got in the car and pulled out of the school parking lot, laughing their asses off.

A few of them went to the mall after the game, and 'Nasia watched how smooth Ke was walking through the mall as if he was untouchable. RahKe was pulling girl's numbers left and right, but she pretended she didn't care what he was doing, or who he was talking to at that moment. Ky'Nasia watched him spit game and play games with the chicks at the mall. It was at that moment that she should've known better. When they left the mall, Ke counted how many numbers he'd gotten and threw them on the ground. His friend, Duck, kept his numbers in his pocket. He didn't get that many numbers anyway and they clowned him most of the ride home.

Ke and 'Nasia talked about how long it was since they had seen each other and what their plans were for the school year.

They kicked it like best friends in the back seat of Big Sis's car. 'Nasia was falling for someone and something she said she'd never wanted, a thug nigga. They kissed and held hands during the ride home from the mall. Then they exchanged numbers and continued talking.

After two weeks, Ke was calling her his girl, so 'Nasia decided to end it with her boyfriend, Malachi. She began attending more of his events and less of her own. The more time they spent together, the more she got to know the real Ke, and she started to see a different side of him. She wanted to back out then, but she was too curious and caught up with what his mouth said rather than the actions she saw.

In the middle of round one, round two began. Ky'Nasia was too caught up and forgot to block with her hands. Instead, she left herself open to the left and right hooks of lying and cheating. And guess what? It hurt like hell when it happened. Ke's lying started to occur daily, so she mentioned it. It died down for a while and things went back to normal. She was his queen again. She grinned while on his arm, and they went to dinner and a movie. She attended the sports events at his school and even dragged her nephew along with her. They were on top of the world, but it didn't last. She could hear the whispering of the other females behind her back. One girl was bold enough to say, "What does he want with that little ass girl? She ain't got shit on us. He needs to let me ride that dick and show him how I get down. My head game strong as hell." They laughed as they stared at the back of her head.

'Nasia listened to them giggling as the game ended. Then she watched as they ran to the courts to be the first ones to touch or say something to Ke, but Ke walked past them as if he had tunnel vision. She laughed to herself as their eyes locked, and he made his way to her. Game over bitches, he still left with her. 'Nasia, being naïve as ever, walked to the car hand and hand with Ke, not knowing that they had slid their numbers in his pocket.

On the drive home, they talked about their plans for the weekend, a beach day. When she got home, she showered and got dressed for bed. Before she could close her eyes, the phone rang, it was Ke's sister. She told 'Nasia about 'her boy' who had just hopped in a car with some chicks. Ky'Nasia tried to shake the thought of him hurting her, but she couldn't help but wonder.

Saturday morning came, and she was ready for their trip to the beach. She sat on the corner of her bed calling Ke back to back. No answer. She started pacing the floor as it got later in the day. Ky'Nasia tried calling him one more time, at three in the afternoon and his mom picked up the phone.

"Girl, this boy is sleeping. He just got in after six this morning. I will tell him to call you when he gets up." She hung up, and the line went dead. Ky'Nasia dropped the phone on the hook as her mind began to race. Six in the morning? Where was he until six in the morning? Bet he was gonna hear her mouth that day.

She changed clothes and put her stuff away, then headed outside to her homegirl's crib to chill and relax her nerves. They sat on the porch playing cards and watching the niggas play ball in the park. It was nice as hell out, so niggas had their shirts off and their ballin' shorts on. Dicks were bouncing everywhere. Ky'Nasia heard her mom yelling her name down the block, so she called home. Her mom told her that her 'little friend' had just called. She rolled her eyes as she hung up the phone. Was he serious? It was 7:45 pm. What beach did he think they were going to? She finished her game of spades, then walked to her house to eat and make a few phone calls. Listening to "Summer Rain" by Carl Thomas on her Walkman, she wolfed down a bowl of rice and beans with fried chicken. Then she ran back up the block.

After the lights turned on in the park, the boys left the courts to take showers. They got fresh and came back out to shoot dice and watch the girls play double dutch. Every girl got her turn jumping rope as the boys made silly comments about their titties when they jumped. The streetlights came on, and it was time for Ky'Nasia to head home. As she got halfway there, she could see RahKe walking up the street. She continued to take her time walking because she was beyond pissed at him. She was so pissed that she walked right past him as if she didn't know him. RahKe grabbed her hand and said, "Baby I am sorry. I should have called you, and I shouldn't have stood you up."

"But you didn't. I ain't beat for these games. I could have made other plans."

"I know. Please let me make it up to you. I said I was sorry."

Going against her better judgment, she allowed RahKe another chance. The following weekend, they made plans to catch a seven o'clock movie. 'Nasia was dressed and ready to go by 6 pm. When she called Ke and his sister, Nikki told her that he already left, she was super hype as she danced in the mirror waiting on him to get there. Ke arrived at her house at 7:25 pm. The movie started at 7:05 pm. Again, 'Nasia was pissed, but she went anyway. They enjoyed the movie, then they went to get ice cream before he took her home. On cloud nine, she hopped in the shower and awaited RahKe to call. He called her, and they talked until the phones died. Those damn cordless phones were a blessing and a curse at the same time. Happy with how her night ended she went to sleep smiling.

Ky'Nasia woke up to a phone call telling her to get ready to go to the boardwalk. Excited, she got dressed as fast as lightning, after a quick shave and shower. The boardwalk was packed. Everybody and their momma were there, meaning there were many chicks that walked up to Ke to say 'hi' as if 'Nasia wasn't standing there. Of course, they were all his 'cousins'. That is until one bold chick tried to kiss him. The look on his face said it all, but 'Nasia's face was twisted. She walked off to cool down and thought to herself, Ke has got some explaining to do. She heard him running up behind her, but the bitch also came over. "Sorry, I didn't know you were his girl. I thought you were a friend like all the rest of us." That made it no better as Ke's hand slapped his face in disbelief of her wack ass apology. Trying to make up for the bullshit, they walked around holding hands and with RahKe's arm around 'Nasia. The statement was clear to everyone, but not to her.

The night came to a stop and 'Nasia got out of the car. Ke rolled the window down and said, "I'll call you in the morning. Hopefully, you'll feel better about yourself. I told you, I don't want those girls. I want you, but you're being dumb. I ain't got time for that bullshit."

Ky'Nasia turned around to curse him out, but he had already rolled up the window and drove off. Steaming mad, she went into the house to get ready for bed. This was going to be a long night, so she took a bubble bath to relax her mind. RahKe had some sort of mind control over her, but she didn't even realize it. She prepared herself for more lies and they came from every angle.

RahKe left events to go to the after-parties but told 'Nasia that his coaches held him late after the game. She later found out that he was out on the block hustlin' too. He dropped off money to her at school so she could get her hair and nails done. Somehow this made up for all the lies he told her all weekend. For a while, she wasn't even disrespected by any other females. He kept himself under the radar for the moment, but things were still rocky, yet calm at the same time.

Ky'Nasia felt like she had a responsibility to play her part and be his peace since she was Ke's girl. She stopped making everything out to be such a big deal and let a lot of shit roll off her back because she was Ke's queen. She fixed her crown a couple of times at a party in Millville, but it wasn't enough. Some chick was all up on RahKe and he gave her his attention like he didn't have a girl. No, he gave her attention like 'Nasia wasn't at the same party. This wasn't a fix your crown moment, so she left to avoid making a scene. When she got to the corner, Ke caught up with her and said,

"You're acting really corny! This is a party and girls are gonna dance with the flyest nigga here. If you're gonna act like a baby every time someone dances with me then go home. If not, come back and relax with your man." As Ke leaned in to kiss her, she could smell the liquor on his breath, it was strong. They walked back to the party with Ke's arm around her waist. Once inside, the other girl was grillin' her hard. She pushed passed 'Nasia as she headed up the stairs. Ky'Nasia looked at RahKe and he flashed that fucking grin at 'Nasia and her heart dropped. They danced with each other for the rest of the party.

The next day, in school, the party chick must've felt some type of way. She approached 'Nasia and they started fighting. That was the wrong thing to do over her man. They both got suspended. All because her man was writing his number on different bitches' hand and souping their heads up!

Round 2

Below the Belt

Round two kicked in midway through the first round with a quick jab to the gut. Ky'Nasia got hit with, "I saw your man with these two girls, late night the other day." She was still trying to avoid all of the 'he-said-she-said' bullshit flying her way, but it was very hard. She couldn't be on every scene or at every party because she was a young Sophomore who was dating an older dude.

Doing her best to keep RahKe happy, she started sneaking out of church to spend more time with him. One Sunday night, while at church, Ke and Tamia pulled up so 'Nasia could see him. She ran out of the church and hopped in the car. She knew she was going to get in trouble, so she decided not to go back to the church at all. 'Nasia needed to see her man. They rode around listening to music and acting all crazy until about ten that night. Afterward, Tamia dropped them off at 'Nasia's house 'cause she had to beat her mom home. They chilled on the steps until about eleven that night, then Ke walked uptown to his aunt's crib. When Ky'Nasia's mom got home, she, of course, put her on punishment. For one month she had to stay inside and learn Bible scriptures because she left the church without permission. To make the time go faster, she wrote letters and mailed them to RahKe. He wrote back a few times and sent drawings of cartoon characters that she loved.

'Nasia got off punishment three weeks later. She could tell Ke was hiding something, but she just wasn't sure what it was at the time. She asked him if he was talking to any other girls, but with a straight face, he said, "No." A few months later, he moved to his aunt's spot in Millville. Ky'Nasia was happy because she thought she would get to see Ke more. Boy was she wrong. His Aunt BB hated her! She would call her names like 'jailbait'. Her kids also called her a stalker. Even until today, Ky'Nasia lives with those names. Whenever she would call the house for Ke, they would hang up on her or say that he wasn't there, when he was. When 'Nasia came to see RahKe, they would leave her standing outside on the steps for hours before letting her in the house or even telling her that he wasn't home. Looking back at it now, it was all a sign that Ky'Nasia wasn't willing to see.

One night, 'Nasia came to see him the day before Valentine's Day, to drop off his gift. It was raining and freezing cold outside. She knocked on the door for twenty minutes before his cousin came to the door and let her in. She didn't stay long because no one there liked her. She handed Ke's stuff to his little sister and left. Two hours later, RahKe called her and thanked her for his gift. They only talked for a little while because he said he was tired.

The next day at school, 'Nasia was called down to the office because she had a delivery. RahKe dropped off 'Nasia gift to her school. She walked around with her balloons tied to her bookbag and held her flowers and other stuff in her hand all day. Nothing could ruin that day for her. Malachi gave her a plastic rose that smelled so good and a letter telling her how he felt about her. When 'Nasia told RahKe about the letter, he told her to throw it away and not to talk to Malachi anymore. She listened like a good girl.

Round two was full of more lies and dishonesty. A few days after Valentine's Day, Ke's sister, Nikki, called. She told 'Nasia that some chick kept calling for Ke and her name was Shanita. She gave 'Nasia the girl's number. She called her up, but Shanita said that she and Ke were just friends, but that she wanted to be more than friends. The nerve of this whore! That's when Ky'Nasia let her know who she was, Ke's girlfriend; and that she should chill out, but she didn't. Instead, she said that Ke told her something different.

"He told me that he didn't have a girl and that we could see where things go if I played my cards right. That's why I call him. I wanna know how to play my cards right."

Ky'Nasia was so hurt. Why would Ke tell another girl to play her cards right? Sitting on her bedroom floor, 'Nasia waited for RahKe to call her, but the phone never rang. She went to bed with a lot on her mind. What should she do? What should she say? Should she even believe this girl?

At school, she was walking around confused and lost. She went through the day hoping her mind would stop racing, but it never did. 'Nasia rushed home after practice and called Ke. RahKe put her on hold but never clicked back over. Tears formed in her eyes as she realized he wasn't going to click over. She did her homework and stayed inside because of the weather, cleaning her room while listening to slow jams. Once finished, she headed for the shower. After dinner, she climbed into the bed to watch *I Love Lucy.* That was her show. The phone rang, it was Ke. She asked how his day went and what had happened to him yesterday. There was some small talk before 'Nasia questioned him about that chick and what he had said to her. The first thing Ke said out of his mouth was, “Here we go with this bullshit. Why is it that every time we talk it’s about some chick? Damn ‘Nasia! She just some bitch I met at the mall a few weeks ago. She’s crazy.”

“How’d she get your number and why’d you give it to her?”

“You’re right. I should have given her a fake number like you do. Plus, I never told her I didn’t have a girl. I said we were on bad terms right now.”

“Why did you lie? We’re not on bad terms, as far as I know.”

“We are, ‘cause you’re always worried about other bitches. Like chill. Damn. I still fuck with you. I don’t want them broads.”

“Whatever yo! That’s bullshit and you know it.”

“Do you miss me or what?”

“You know I miss you.”

“Good ‘cause I miss you, too. I will be out there tomorrow when you get out of school. Go to my aunt’s house. I love you.”

“Okay. I love you, too.”

She hung up the phone and flipped all over the bed. Her heart jumped a thousand times. She was smiling so hard, her cheeks were hurting. She let go of all the anger she had in her heart towards Ke because he loved her.

After school, ‘Nasia raced to get uptown to Ke’s aunt’s house. She got there right as he was getting out of the car. They walked into the house and straight to the living room. They ordered Chinese food and watched movies until it got dark out.

Then, they sat on the couch kissing and hugging until it was time for her to go home. RahKe kissed her with so much passion and power, and his tongue game was no joke. Ky'Nasia nutted on herself just from kissing him as his hands caressed her body. Thank God it was time for her to go home because she was losing her mind on that couch!

She called a cab and got dropped off at home. Still hot and bothered she decided to take a nice hot bath. While in the tub, she played her favorite songs by Jagged Edge and Dru Hill. 'Nasia let the hot water rush over her body. She placed one leg on each side of the tub as the warm water hit her pussy. A slight moan escaped her mouth. She slid her fingers down her breast and played with her nipples as waves of hot water banged up against her sweet pussy. She put one hand in her caramel square and slid her fingers in and out while rocking her hips. With her eyes closed, she thought about the way Ke kissed and touched her on the couch. Shock waves struck 'Nasia's body as she played with her clit faster. She felt her nut coming, so she used one hand to squeeze her nipples and the other to fuck her pussy hard and fast. She nutted in the tub. Her body sunk into the water as she released herself. She quickly let the water out and took a shower. She dried off in her room as flashes of RahKe holding her ran through her mind, but she was snapped out of it at the sound of her mom yelling, "Phone 'Nasia!" Happy he called, she grabbed the phone and jumped in the bed naked. That was the start of her sleeping without clothes on. She laid in bed naked on the phone with him for an hour. By the end of the call, she was telling Ke how bad she wanted him and how horny she was. Laughing at how she was reacting to him, Ke told her, "We'll make something happen." The 'I love you's' hit the air as they hung up.

Floating on her own high, she went to school a new woman. Ky'Nasia was beyond happy and nothing was going to change that. She finished art class and ran into her friend Tamia. They made plans for 'Nasia to come over that weekend. They talked about their men as they walked to class. Mia was crushing on Big Mack hard. She talked about him all the time. School let out and 'Nasia headed home. The weather was finally warming up, so she was ready to hit the streets. She did her homework, finished her chores, and sped down the sidewalk to her girl's crib to catch up with her and play jump rope. She played a few rounds of double dutch before she headed home to get ready for bed. Entering the house, Ky'Nasia sat down and had dinner. Then she ran up the stairs to take her shower. She asked her mom about going to Tamia's house for the weekend. Of course, she said yes. After showering, she hopped into bed and made her phone calls. She hit Ke's line last because they always stayed on the phone the longest. RahKe answered the phone on the first ring talking shit.

"Why are you just now calling me? I was going to come out there and see you today, but I didn't hear from you until now."

"I thought you had track practice today. I am sorry. You know I want to see you."

"You want me to touch that body?"

"Yes sir, I do."

"I want to too. I want to suck on them big ass titties while fingering your pussy."

"I want to feel that shit right now. Don't start with me. You're making me horny," she said in a soft sweet voice.

"Can I play with your pussy the next time I see you?"

"Yes, baby."

With her hands on her nipples, she pushed them up to her

mouth. Licking on one nipple at a time she whispered, "I want you so bad."

"What do you want from me?"

"I want you to play with this pussy while sucking on my titties. I want you to slide your hands around my waist while you lick my nipples, hold my hips tight, and lick my bellybutton."

"Can I plant small kisses on the inner part of your thighs and flick my tongue in the creases? Am I allowed to stick my finger in the caramel center? Can I rub my fingers across your clit until you lose your mind?"

"Damn, baby I want you right now! You got my pussy so wet."

"Do me a favor and play with it for me."

She slipped her fingers into her already wet pussy. Soft moans drifted out into the air. The radio played gently in the background as she explained, "This feels so good. I can't wait until it's you that's touching me. I want to feel you. It's driving me crazy. Ah!"

"You got my dick hard as a rock. I want to lick the back of your neck as my hands run across your ass. I want to squeeze your cheeks as I rub my dick between your ass cheeks."

"Shit baby, you got me ready to bust everywhere."

"Good! Let me hear that pussy talk. Can you make it talk for me?"

She put the phone close to her pussy so he could hear the juices from her pussy splashing up against her hand. That shit was so loud and super wet. Her moans grew louder as she hit her peak.

She fingered her pussy faster and harder. She slammed her hand into her g-spot until she lost control. Her body shook as she climaxed and nutted all over her hand and damn near on the phone. Barely able to breathe, she put the phone to her ear, "That was crazy. What did you do to me? It felt so good.

'Nasia listened to Ke's breathing change as he stroked his dick faster and harder. "You like the way I play with that pussy, huh? You got my dick hard as hell."

"I need to feel you so bad that my pussy is throbbing."

"I want to smack it on your ass. Can I beat your ass with my dick? I want to stick it in your pussy.

"I want you inside me. You got me over here shaking and shit."

"Can I stroke your pussy nice and slow from the back while you wind your hips on this dick?"

"Yes, baby. Slide that dick in this pussy. It's soaking wet for you. Can you hold my hips while I slow grind on that dick?"

"Can I fuck this pussy?"

"Grab these ass cheeks and jam that dick in this pussy."

"Is this my pussy? Tell Daddy this is his pussy."

"Daddy, this is your pussy. Fuck me, baby. Take it. It's yours." I rubbed my hands all over my pussy and it was soaking wet. I heard him working his dick hard as hell. I softly say, "Fuck this pussy."

"Shit, I just fucking busted on this couch and I ain't got nothing out here to clean this shit up with. Do you see what you made me do? Let me clean this mess up."

She also got up and cleaned herself up. They talked about their plans to hit the club on the weekend and made plans to go to dinner on Friday after his track meet. She got comfortable in the bed as Ke got ready to take his shower. They said their goodnights, 'I love you's', and then went to bed.

Smiling from ear to ear, she prepared for the weekend with her king. Ky'Nasia shaved everything! She made sure she had new panties for each day she was going to see him. They were going to see the movie, *The Matrix*, and she needed to be on point for her man.

Weekend ready, she danced all the way to her house after school. 'Nasia grabbed the phone and called Tamia to see what time she was picking her up. Mia came through and got her at 5:30 pm. They went and picked up their dudes and headed to Red Lobster. They ate and talked shit to each other. Then, they put their plans in motion for going to the club on Saturday night. She had already packed her best clothes and shoes to hit the club. They decided to walk the mall until it closed. It felt good spending time with her man. They dropped Ke off at his aunt's crib and then headed to Tamia's house.

The next day, they cleaned the house. Getting their chores done was a must for them to go out later that night. They danced in the mirrors as they cleaned up the house and got their moves ready that night. They did everything early and chilled until it was time to get ready to go. After they made sure each other's hair and outfits were on point, they went on their way to pick up the fellas. As they headed for the club, they laid down the rules.

No leaving the club with other people and always leave with who you came with. No passing out their phone numbers. No hands in places that they shouldn't be. Lastly, always find each other thirty minutes before the club closes.

Once inside the club, they went their separate ways. Watching the dance floor as people flooded the doors, they vibed to the music. Mia and 'Nasia hit the dance floor when "*Back That Ass Up*" came on. Popping that ass like it was nobody business, some guy came and stood behind Ky'Nasia. RahKe was dancing next to her with a girl that was too big for him, and he couldn't handle her. He was stepping all over 'Nasia's feet. Using her shoulders to hold himself up, 'Nasia stepped off. The guy followed close behind. When the song was over Ke made his way to her. After telling 'ole boy that he needed to fall back, they walked to the slow jam room and danced with each other. Ending their night in each other's arms, the lights came on and they headed to the car.

The drive from Cherry Hill was jumping. They were in the back seat getting busy. RahKe's hands were all over the place and so was Ky'Nasia's. They kissed and made out the entire ride to Denny's. Ke kissed all down her neck and chest. RahKe unsnapped her bra as she unbuttoned his pants. Seeing how hard and big his dick was her mouth dropped open. She stroked it slowly. He sucked on her titties and fingered her pussy at the same time. She was so ready for him to put it in, but she wanted it to be the right time and the right place. They got each other all hot and bothered, but didn't go all the way that night. They left things to their imagination in preparation for the next time.

At Denny's, they ate and had a good time. He told her not to make him have to fuck up none of them niggas in the club. They laughed and enjoyed their food. Their night came to an end as the girls took them home. They kissed and said their 'goodnights'.

A few weeks later they were at Aunt BB's crib chilling and watching TV. They played a few games of cards before heading up the stairs to chill. They sat on the couch and began kissing and holding hands. Everyone was downstairs, so they made their way to the floor. Ke pulled the covers over his head as he lifted up her shirt. Pulling her bra straps down and unhooking it in the back, he licked her nipple as it escaped the bra. Nervous and scared, RahKe asked, “Are you ready? You sure you wanna do this?” Ky’Nasia shook her head yes and he continued to suck on her breasts. Feeling herself getting wet she reached for his dick. It was hard as a brick. She squeezed it firmly and stroked it gently. RahKe slid his hands down her stomach and right into her caramel square. Without warning a moan escaped her lips. He smiled and bit his bottom lip. Chills shot down her spine as her legs automatically went into an open frog position. They played with each other’s hotspots for a few minutes more. She begged to feel him inside her, so Ke slowly climbed on top of her. Easing it in, he pushed his body up against hers. As it entered her heaven, a small shout of pain left her mouth. It hurt like hell. RahKe asked if Ky’Nasia wanted him to stop. She shook her head no. Double-checking, he asked again, while working his hips slowly in and out of her. It felt so good but hurt at the same damn time. After she got used to the groove of it, it felt amazing. That pussy was so wet, and she was able to throw it back a little bit. In the middle of them fucking, everyone decided to come upstairs to watch TV. They were stuck on the floor with the covers over their heads with Ke’s dick inside Ky’Nasia. After a few minutes of them not moving or talking, everyone got the hint and went to the other side of the attic. They finished what they had started, and there was no looking back after that. Having RahKe inside her was a must!

Tamia picked ‘Nasia up after she got off of work, and they went to Tamia’s spot. While taking a shower, flashbacks of her night flooded her mind. Damn, she really enjoyed herself. It felt good, and she really wanted it. ‘Nasia’s mind was stuck on how RahKe made her body feel. She loved him even more for being gentle with her. He did everything nice and gentle. He never rushed her. She smiled from ear to ear that night.

The next week she was at the mall and heard someone calling her name. When she turned around, she saw that it was Nikki. She never came with good news. 'Nasia asked her, "What's up?" She didn't disappoint. She told her that Ke was kicking it with some chick from around the way. Trying to not let that piss her off, Ky'Nasia did some more shopping. She was drained from trying not to be pissed, so she headed home and hit the shower. No need to wait on his call because she knew it wasn't coming. It was a Saturday, Summer night, but 'Nasia quickly drifted off to sleep.

Round 3

Sucker Punched

Ding! Ding! The bell sounds again for round three. There was so much hurt and pain in this round and the strikes only grew stronger. Some 'girl from around the way' turned out to be a chick from the hood, someone 'Nasia knew all too well. She had issues with this girl from a previous relationship. It was crazy that RahKe would be talking to this particular chick! Two rounds at a time ain't fair, but rule number one: NEVER fuck with a bitch that was from the same county or hood as Queen Ky'Nasia.

Her junior year of high school was about to start, and she was rushing around getting things ready for school. 'Nasia had to make sure her grades were great because she had plans to go away for college and to live on campus. She put all of her focus on school. She found out which colleges offered the best education for her career choice, started touring local colleges, and going on trips to different out of state colleges. Excited, she told Ke all the things that the colleges had to offer, but he was only concerned that she might have plans to leave him. Of course, her answer was no, despite how his actions had made her feel broken and scared.

Ky'Nasia's birthday was the first Friday of the beginning

school week. She made plans with Ke to go to dinner and then see the movie *Swimfan.* All week they talked about what she should do to her hair, and what she was going to wear. Each day she was more and more excited about what was going to happen on her birthday. She was turning the big sixteen, so her mom allowed her to stay out until 11:30 pm that night. Thursday, after school, her friends took her to the mall to find an outfit for her to wear on her date. She got a short red dress with black flowers and some black sandals. She went to the nail salon and got her eyebrows, nails, and feet done. It was a great way to start off her birthday weekend. After a long day of shopping and pampering, she took a shower and hit the sheets.

As her eyes began to close, the phone rang. Jumping out of her skin, she grabbed the phone and said, "Hello?" It was RahKe. He had called to confirm their plans for tomorrow and to see if there was anything else she needed to do before they met up at the mall. They spent the night talking to each other about their day and how much they missed each other. As the yarns continued to be exchanged, they fell asleep on the phone. Waking up to the buzzing sound of her dead phone at 4:45 am, she placed it on the charger, and went back to sleep.

In class, Ky'Nasia received birthday shout outs from everyone. A few people got her balloons and candy. She received a free cookie at lunch and even got to get out of gym for the day. Things were working out in her favor, and she was determined to enjoy her birthday. At the end of the day, her teacher pulled her into a classroom to let her know that she was one of the kids selected to go to an interview at Rowan University for their Education Opportunity Fund program. This was going to help her with finances for college. She was so happy, but she didn't want to tell Ke and ruin her birthday plans. So, she kept the good news to herself.

Once she got home from school, she showered and shaved. She laid across her bed naked thinking about what was next for them if she went off to school. She awoke from her daydream to the sound of her mom calling her, asking if she was ready to be dropped off because she was leaving. 'Nasia rushed to finish getting ready. She curled her hair and pinned it up into a bun. She sprayed the perfume that RahKe loved and ran down the stairs. Getting into the van, her mom told her the rules to her again, and they both agreed that if she was late, she would be punished.

Jumping out of the van 'Nasia headed into the mall, but there was no sign of RahKe at their meeting spot. Ky'Nasia continued to wait for Ke. Looking at the clock again, she became upset that it was 6:45 pm and he still wasn't there. She went to the payphone to call Ke's house. She was told that he hadn't been there since he got out of school. As she walked back to the meeting spot, she saw Ke walking up. It was 7:15 pm. There was no time for dinner since the movie started at 7:50 pm. 'Nasia was a little disappointed since she hadn't eaten all day because she was waiting to go to Red Lobster.

They headed straight to the movies and got their tickets and some snacks. The movie theater was type packed, but mostly in the middle and front. They sat all the way in the back far corner, away from everyone. As they took their seats, Ke told her how beautiful she was, and how happy he was to see her. She smiled and told Ke the same even though he was late.

When the movie started, RahKe wrapped his arms around her and held her while they watched most of the movie. Midway through the movie, Ke lifted her dress to see if she wore the panties he had asked her to wear. He ran his hand across the top of her pussy. She looked at him and smiled. That grin appeared on his face, and it was curtains from there. He pulled her closer to him and whispered in her ear, "I wanna touch it." RahKe slid his hand up and down her pussy until the front of her panties were wet. She was hot and ready to be touched. He took off his jacket and laid it across her, then lifted her dress higher so he could see her titties. They were sitting there so perfect without a bra on. Ke lowered his mouth to her nipples and kissed them both. He continued to rub her pussy as he began to suck on her nipples. She was trying her best to watch the movie, but her body was jonesing for him. 'Nasia put her head back and let out a soft moan as his fingers managed to slide inside her panties. "Take them panties off," he said, but she was nervous, so he did it for her. They kissed and played with each other until the movie was over. They left the movies with 'Nasia's panties in his pocket, and she went to the bathroom to clean up. They walked to Burger King to grab something to eat while waiting for the bus.

On the bus, Ke told her to come over his house and that he would get her a cab home. She listened and got off the bus with him to go to his aunt's house. They went straight up the stairs and into the back room. No one but the cat was home. RahKe made a pallet on the floor and they laid on it. He lifted her dress over her head and dropped it to the floor. His hands were so warm as they grabbed her titties and pushed them both into his mouth. It felt good as he was squeezing and sucking on her titties, but it was time to go. "It's getting late Ke. I have to get ready to go." His hands kept moving and made their way down to her caramel center to start working magic.

"The boss ain't ready for you to go yet. I'm gonna give you what you want before you go." Ky'Nasia asked if he had a condom, but Ke said, "You know I shoot blanks. I can't have any kids. We've been here before, and ain't nothing happened yet."

So dumb and naïve, she allowed Ke to fuck the shit out of

her raw. He started off slow and gentle, but the more she told him she had to go, the rougher he got. Pulling her hips toward him, he flipped her over and fucked her doggie-style. She felt his soul leave his body as the cab driver pulled up and Ke nutted inside her. Putting her panties back on, she ran down the steps to hold the cab. There was no time to clean up. She hopped in the cab with her panties to the side. She tried to avoid all the nut draining out of her to get onto her panties. That didn't work. As she pulled up in front of her house, her mom said, "You're punished for a week because you're late and you didn't catch the bus home." Still on cloud nine, she went to her room and got ready to take a shower. She called RahKe and told him what happened. He told her that she was his 'Queen' and nothing would keep them apart. She believed him and went to bed feeling like a billion bucks. Ke always had that effect on her.

A week later she was off punishment and hit the mall and football games hard. Watching all of the guys get hurt during the game made her kinda sad, so they all went to the mall the next day for some relaxation. RahKe bought her a few things, and himself a few things too. As they shopped, 'Nasia noticed that some girl was following them around the mall, so she asked Ke who she was. He pretended not to know, but she could tell he was lying.

They decided to go to Red Lobster and ate dinner. He was such a gentleman when he wanted to be. They laughed, talked, held hands, and kissed. They left and waited for the bus, but some girls tried to jump her at the bus stop. Ke held 'Nasia back and protected her even though she was down for the fight. He always made her feel special and she believed she was safe when she was with him. On the bus ride home, they talked about their forever plans, their plans to be together until death do they part. Just them two! That was the plan anyway. They reached BB's house and her mom was there to pick her up. They kissed goodnight and she went home. She showered and got ready for bed. Ke called about an hour later telling her that he went looking for the dudes that were with those girls. They talked about it for a while and then went to bed.

On September 22nd, at 6:30 am, Ky'Nasia began another fight while still in the third round. While in the bathroom, she begged God to allow her period to 'just be late' as long as it still came. There were no cramps and no period. She called RahKe and let him know that they had a problem. Ke told her to relax and give it another day or two. To get out of school, she told her mom that her stomach hurt and that she had bad cramps. This gave her time to come up with a master plan on how to get her period back before anyone noticed that she didn't have a period that month. The weekend hit and her period still hadn't come. She sat in the bathroom trying to figure out a way to fix the mess they'd created. She missed two more days of school hoping that things would change and that her life would go back to normal, but it didn't. She was pregnant. She called Ke to tell him, and that she wasn't keeping the baby. She was too young to have a baby! Her mother was going to kill them, and she didn't want to ruin the opportunity she had to go away to college. Listening to Ky'Nasia freak out, he yelled, "You're not killing my baby!" Her jaw hit the floor.

"What do you mean I'm not killing your baby? Newsflash, I'm sixteen years old, a junior in high school with plans to live on campus at college. I'm not even supposed to be having SEX! It's our baby and neither one of us are ready to be parents." They hung up and she went back to her bedroom to lay down.

Opening her eyes to the sound of Ke calling her from downstairs, she rolled out of bed. She went downstairs to meet Ke and he took her to the back step to talk. He wanted to do some research on abortions before they made their decision. She agreed to let him ask around before they made any moves, but Ke didn't do any research because he wanted the baby. Instead, he told the world that he was going to be a dad. She made plans twice to get an abortion without telling Ke, but both plans fell through. No one wanted to help her do something she might later regret.

In October, the morning sickness started to kick her ass. She was getting sick all day, every day. The crazy thing is that halfway through the month, her period came, but only lasted for three days. This made her buy a pregnancy test. POSITIVE. She was sick! For the month of November, she tried putting pads in the trash to keep everyone from knowing and it worked. Her stomach started to get a little shape and her sickness was getting worse with everything that her mom cooked. She knew she was going to have to tell her soon.

December rolled around and it was over. Her god-sister and god-mom, Tiff and Stacy, somehow found out. Tiff was hurt because 'Nasia wanted to get an abortion. They refused to let her get one and made her tell her mom, who then told Ke's mom, after she beat 'Nasia's hands with a metal spoon. That night was a nightmare. She was glad the secret was out but was hurt by all the pain and disappointment she had caused her family. She was supposed to be different. She was the one that should have gotten her mother out of the hood.

The third-round left Ky'Nasia wounded, and pregnant at sixteen. Damn, this was going to be rough! Her family was talking trash about her and Ke. They knew he was cheating on her. They made comments like, "She'll be stuck on welfare because he isn't going to help her with the baby" and "He'll leave her all stressed out and worried because she's pregnant and can't take care of herself." More punches rolled in as they began talking about Shanita. She tried ignoring their whispers, but they just got louder.

When she went for her doctor's appointment, the doctor said, "You have to stop stressing and try to relax before you lose the baby." Relax? That's what you say to a junior in high school with no job or means to make ends meet for herself or a baby? Despite how she felt, she tried to make things better for herself. She put all of her focus on school. She stopped chasing Ke and let him be great, but he was still her man and the father of her child, so she had to stay close. She talked to him off and on and gave him updates about the baby. She always went to her appointments alone or with her mom. Ke was around but absent at the same time. It hurt like hell. The reason he wanted the baby wasn't clear, but one thing she could say was that he took care of her cravings. She ate Pizza Hut wings, crabs, and mall pizza daily. Her baby continued to grow. Towards the end of the pregnancy, RahKe started to come around more, and his family finally accepted her baby as part of their own.

Round 4

Rolling with the Punches

The fourth-round swung into gear with a gut striking kick. Ky'Nasia was sitting on her mom's lap crying. RahKe's cousin, Nylah, had just told her that Ke already had a two-week-old baby girl! She was still pregnant with what was supposed to be his first child! 'Nasia's mom told her not to worry and that she would be okay. She got herself together as she accepted Ke's call. He called to tell his six-month pregnant 'girlfriend' that he had a baby by some girl who was supposed to have been a one-night stand. Did this nigga really love her? She couldn't believe he did her like that. Shit, that hurt! She could no longer breathe, or stand, so she went to bed.

The next day was a blur. Ke's mom called her to talk about the situation. She did her best to ease 'Nasia's mind and to make sure she'd still let RahKe be involved in the baby's life. Though she was extremely hurt and broken, she agreed. She never wanted her child to grow up without a father anyway. Ke's mom invited her to come over for a BBQ and to pick out the theme for the baby's room. After catching a bus to Vineland, she waited at the Rite Aid for his mom to pick her up. The food was already on the grill when they got to the house. RahKe walked out of the house to help her and his mom up the stairs. Once in the house, Ky'Nasia went straight to his mom's room and sat on the bed. Ke and his little sister, Aimee, followed her asking a bunch of questions that she had no plans on answering for either one of them. Finally, after avoiding RahKe most of the night, it was time to eat. He made her plate and begged her to talk to him. She looked at him with tears in her eyes as he grabbed her face for a kiss. She turned her head away.

"Can I please explain? I am so sorry, and I never meant to hurt you or cause you any pain. I was being stupid. All drunk up, thinking I was cool! I don't want anybody but you. You're my Queen and I love you."

He reached for her face again, but Ky'Nasia walked away. Knowing that he and that girl had a history together was making her very upset! Every time Ke touched her, she felt sick. 'Nasia ate a little of the food and was ready to go home. She waited for her ride to come at 11:30 pm, but they never showed up. Now she was stuck out there with no ride home and she had a doctor's appointment in the morning. She called her mom to let her know what was going on, and she said she would pick her up in the morning. She went to Ke mom's room and laid down. Of course, like a sick puppy, he followed. Ke took 'Nasia shoes off and massaged her feet. They were pretty swollen from walking and standing all day. She asked him to leave her alone, and he began to tell her how much he needed her and how he wouldn't make it without her. RahKe told her that he would never again cause the pain that he saw in her eyes. Oh, how she wished that was true. She ended up crying herself to sleep in Ke's arms.

The next morning, he went to school, and she was left there with Nikki. She cooked breakfast for them but ate most of it.

Ky'Nasia ended up eating only two french toast and a half cup of orange juice. Like really? She wasn't the one that was pregnant. Nikki had the nerve to tell 'Nasia that she didn't eat enough food to get a big cup of juice. She watched Nikki play on the computer until her mom arrived, who came just in time for her doctor's appointment. The checkup went well, and everything was fine with the baby. She got her notes from school and the date of when her last day of school would be.

Ky'Nasia returned to school the next day and everyone wanted to know how she was doing. The whole time she was pregnant only a hand full of people at the school knew. She participated in gym and everything. She didn't miss a beat! She finally went to the nurse's office and got her pass that said she could eat small snacks and drink fluids in the classroom and go to the restroom when needed. She was seven and a half months by then. Her teachers were upset because they had to keep telling her she couldn't go to the bathroom until she had finished her work. She still didn't tell any of her teachers that she was pregnant. She waited as long as she could to tell them. They didn't know she was pregnant or that she had a pass until one day Ky'Nasia took off her hoodie and asked to go to the bathroom. Before her teacher could say, 'No,' 'Nasia turned around and handed her the pass. When she saw her belly, her jaw hit the floor and 'Nasia ran to the bathroom. When she got back, her teacher was standing in the hall waiting for her.

"What's wrong," 'Nasia asked her crying teacher.

"Why didn't you tell me? How far along are you?"

"I'm eight and a half months pregnant. My last day of school is May 28th." That was only two weeks away. She just kept staring at 'Nasia and shaking her head. She hugged her and told her to get in the classroom. Then, she asked the class who knew that 'Nasia was pregnant and why didn't they tell her. Only three people raised their hands. She told them the highest grade they could get for the class was a B since they liked keeping secrets. They all laughed and finished their work.

While eight and a half months pregnant, her family decided they were taking their family road trip to Florida. It was cool 'cause Ky'Nasia was used to the ride, but with a baby inside of her and so close to her due date, her mom was nervous. They had all her medical paperwork concerning her pregnancy in a backpack in the trunk of the car just in case. They hit the road at 12 am on a Sunday morning. It was a smooth trip there. They only had to stop one time due to an unexpected feeling of nausea. They pulled over so 'Nasia could go to the bathroom, eat something, and get herself together. They finally arrived in Florida, and it was super hot! Everyone got settled in their rooms as they unloaded the cars. Ky'Nasia had a big bed, and she was loving it. Her feet were swollen from being in the car for so long and not being able to elevate them. She relaxed in the room while everyone else went to Walmart to get food.

They enjoyed the palm trees, and the hot weather while they could. She went to several theme parks with her nephew. They walked and rode lots of rides. Every night her feet were swollen from being on them all day. She was huge and all belly walking around Florida, but her weight was still down. She got back from Florida just in time for her doctor appointment and her last few days of school.

On May 24th, she went to the store with her mom to get a bunch of stuff like juice, chips, and ice. When she asked her mom what the stuff was for, she told her that it was for an event she was having at the center that day at 4 pm. As she left the store, her head and back started hurting, so she went home and laid down.

At 3:45 pm, her mom called the house and asked her to come to the center for a few minutes. Ky'Nasia told her she'd be there, but she never got up. Later, she heard a knock at the door. It was Ke telling her, "Get dressed and come on! Your mom told me to come and get you out of bed and take you down to the center." Walking down the street, he reached over and rubbed her belly. "You look like you're ready to pop."

"I feel ready to pop, and I have a headache."

They walked into the center, and it turned out to be her surprise baby shower. RahKe's mom and Ky'Nasia's mom had planned the baby shower and no one even told her. RahKe attended the baby shower off and on. Being the only guy there wasn't his thing. Ky'Nasia's brother popped in for a few minutes and that was all it took for Ke to be out. Her brother promised he would bring Ke right back as they slid out the door. 'Nasia was like, "Whatever," because she had to be there until it was over either way. It was her baby shower. People continued to come in and bring gifts. The food was good, and they played lots of games. 'Nasia got everything she wanted for her baby girl!

After the baby shower was over, RahKe, all high, walked to Ky'Nasia house. Her mom snapped on him because he didn't help carry the gifts into the house. Ke took the stuff to her room and put it away. He told her he was going to a party that night so he would call her in the morning. Later on, she started to get uncomfortable with not being able to hear from him so close to having the baby. She went down the steps to see if her brother was home so he could tell her where Ke was at, but he was passed out on the floor asleep. Ky'Nasia got back in the bed and heard the code call from Ke. She smiled and called Ke back. RahKe let her know that he was home and that he was coming over around 10 am to put the baby stuff together. They said their 'I love you's' and went to bed.

The next morning, RahKe didn't show up at 10 am. She started to worry because her due date was less than a week away and her room was loaded with boxes. She tried calling, but of course, his phone was off. She called around to try and find him but was unsuccessful. 'Nasia went to bed that night angry.

Her last day of school came quickly. Her morning sickness was back, and she was feeling big and pregnant. Ky'Nasia couldn't keep anything down. She lost more weight than she had gained. She walked in her history class, and there were balloons and cake on the front desk. The teacher gave her a baby shower. It was very nice. She got a lot of stuff. They put it in the office until the end of the day because she had six more classes to attend. She went to all of her classes, but when she got to her English class, there was another baby shower for her. Her baby was blessed with lots of gift cards and baby supplies. She had to call her mom to pick her up because she had too much stuff to ride the bus home. Her friends helped her load all the stuff into the car. They hugged and said their 'See you later's'. She waved bye as the car pulled away from the curb. Ky'Nasia got dropped off to Ke's aunt's house and of course, he wasn't there. That had her flaming hot. She walked back across town to her older brother's crib to wait for her mom to pick her up, who dropped her off home and then left for church.

After eating a bowl of chocolate chip cookie dough ice cream, Ky'Nasia started putting her baby's bassinet together. She started watching Comic View, but was dozing off. She ended up falling asleep on the sofa. 'Nasia's mom woke her up at 1:30 am and told her to go get in the bed. She left everything downstairs, showered, and then went to bed. She was in her bed and all of a sudden she felt like she had to poop. She jumped up to go sit on the toilet. Nothing. ‘Nasia laid down, but it hit her again. This time she just turned over. Not knowing she was in labor, she headed downstairs to tell her mom.

“I feel like I have to poop but nothing is coming out. My pains are coming every five to six minutes, but only when I lay down.”

She said, “Well maybe you’re in labor. I am gonna call the hospital and see what they want you to do. Go take a shower in the meantime.”

“I just got out of the shower and my stomach hurts! I ain’t getting back in the tub!”

“The doctors said head into the hospital when contractions are five minutes apart and after showering.”

Ky’Nasia hopped in the shower again with an attitude. She could barely stand up when the next contraction hit her. She was throwing up in the shower as she was washing up. Thank God it was only juice and water that she was throwing up! Her mom helped her get dressed as they called Ke’s uncle’s phone to let RahKe know that ‘Nasia was on her way to the hospital. She got in the car to go to the hospital, but her mom pulled over at Ke’s aunt’s house to try to pick him up. ‘Nasia was so mad.

“Mom come on! We don’t have time for this! I need to get to the hospital. My contractions are now three minutes apart, and we’re still in Millville. Just go! He will have to come later!” She pulled off blowing the horn like a crazy person hoping somebody in there would hear it and wake Ke up. No use, no one heard it.

They arrived at the hospital at 5:32 am. The staff put her in a room and strapped a monitor to her stomach. She had a really big problem with that. She was in pain and it was hurting her, so she took it off. The doctor came and checked her cervix and said, "You are ready to push!"

Ky'Nasia asked, " Can I go use the bathroom first?"

"Make it quick. That baby is coming!"

The bathroom felt so good. It was warm and the floors were heated. After trying to use the bathroom and nothing coming out, she got on the bathroom floor with a few towels to lay down to keep warm. The nurses came in the bathroom, got her up from the floor, put her back on the monitor, and gave her oxygen because she was low. Her contractions were less than one minute apart. The doctor came back, and she checked her cervix again. This time a gush of water came flooding out of her. 'Nasia was mad because she thought she had peed herself. The doctor grabbed her hand and said, "It's time to push. You're having your baby now. That was your water breaking." As the doctor was talking, the nurses set up a mirror so that Ky'Nasia could watch herself give birth, but she kicked it down. The doctor then said, "Take a deep breath and on the next contraction push as hard as you can until I tell you to stop!" It was 5:48 am and she was cold and tired, but she did as she was told, and she pushed. As she pushed, she felt her ass getting hot. It felt like she had to shit, so she asked about the bathroom and they told her to go on the bed. Ky'Nasia's first thought was 'They're bugging. That's nasty.'

Another contraction hit and they all yelled, "Push!" She felt something squeezing out of her vagina. The doctor grabbed her hand and let her feel the baby's head. It was crowning. Disgusted and excited at the same time, she moved her hand and she continued to push until the head was out. The nurses were all around her. They were suctioning the baby as another contraction hit, but the doctor said, "Don't push. Just breathe." Ky'Nasia breathed. On the next contraction, they told her again, "Don't push! Just breathe." Now she was worried. Her God-mom was at the foot of the bed trying to record. Ky'Nasia told her to stop and take the camera out of the room.

Then the next contraction hit, but she fought the urge to push. That was hard! The next contraction came, and she pushed the shoulders out. The hard part was over, and her baby girl was here at 5:53 am. Her beautiful baby was five pounds, six ounces, and nineteen and a half inches long. She named her ZahNyah. Her eyes were so wide, and they were looking all around. The staff tried to give 'Nasia the baby, but being a germaphobe, she yelled, "Clean that thing off first. Don't put that bloody thing on me!" Everyone looked shocked. 'Nasia's mom informed them, "That's just how she is." The last contraction hit, and the placenta was out. The nursing team cleaned her up a little so she could get some rest and bond with the baby. Reality hit again, Ky'Nasia's princess was born! Daddy's little girl was here. She was a blessing. Her mom called Ke's mom to let them know that 'Nasia gave birth and all was well. RahKe's mom cried and screamed with excitement. She promised to come and visit the baby after work, and that she would get in touch with Ke to let him know.

Still sitting on those nasty sheets, Ky'Nasia decided to go take a shower. She didn't want to wait for a nurse to help her. They had taken the baby to do all of the tests and to clean her up the right way. She climbed out of bed and clawed her way to the shower, back to the warm place. She got to the bathroom and the room started spinning. She sat on the floor of the shower with a towel under her butt. The blood poured out of her as the hot water hit her body. It felt so good to be in that shower. 'Nasia washed up and the nurse walked into the bathroom telling her the things she wasn't supposed to do and that she should have called for help. She continued to wash up. She noticed that Ky'Nasia washed her pussy like ten times, so she informed her that the blood wasn't going to stop. She said that 'Nasia would bleed for about two to three weeks until her body healed from labor. She assisted her out of the shower and into a chair. While she changed 'Nasia's bed sheets, 'Nasia dried off and put on some clothes. Ky'Nasia was so sleepy. After putting her in a fresh, clean bed, she gave her a pad with ice in it and told her it would help with the swelling and also slow down some of the bleeding. She taught her how to massage her belly to prevent blood clots and a bulging fundus. She gave her all the aftercare information she needed. She had already called her friends and sent them a picture of her baby.

Ky'Nasia was in that room until 8:20 am. Drifting off to sleep they moved her into another room, the recovery room. As soon as they put her in the room, they brought her the baby. It was time to feed ZahNyah. Ky'Nasia gave her the bottle, and ZahNyah tried to drink it all. It was only two ounces. 'Nasia burped her baby, but she still threw up. They told 'Nasia to give her an ounce next time, then burp her, and then let her have more if she wants it. She agreed. They left ZahNyah in the room with her. ZahNyah had jet black, big, round eyes that never seemed to close. 'Nasia was scared to look in her eyes for too long. She dozed off with ZahNyah in her arms as her breakfast tray was dropped off. The nurse came in and placed the baby girl in the crib next to 'Nasia and told her not to sleep with the baby in the bed. After breakfast, she heard a knock at the door. It was RahKe's mother. She came right in and prepared herself to get 'Dodah,' her nickname for the baby. She held her for a few minutes, then let 'Nasia know she would be back after work, but she just had to see her grandbaby. She was there for a half-hour then went back to work.

Ky'Nasia had the baby in her arms as she was watching TV and dozed off again. When the nurse came in to check on the baby again, and she told her the same thing. She watched 'Nasia feed the baby, but the baby still threw up. This was cause for some concern, so the nurse did a full assessment. After getting her results, she realized the baby's temperature was dropping, so she took the baby to the nursery. 'Nasia asked her to let her know what was going on. The nurse said, "I will send the doctor in to talk with you."

Ky'Nasia was nervous, but not too bad, and fell asleep while watching the news. Later on, one of her friends walked in, it was Lashae asking, "Where's your baby. I went to the nursery looking for her, and she's not in her crib and not in here with you." Now Ky'Nasia was nervous. She called to the nurse's station and in walked the doctor. She stated that she previously came to talk to 'Nasia, but she was sleeping, and she didn't want to wake her. Heated, 'Nasia asked her what was going on. The doctor explained that the baby wasn't holding any food and that her temperature was too low and it wasn't coming back up. They had to put the baby in the NICU. Ky'Nasia was sad. She had already received bad news about her baby girl and RahKe didn't even know she was born yet. They told her that she had to scrub in to go see the baby and only parents and grandparents were allowed in the NICU. Only two people were allowed in the NICU at one time. That made 'Nasia mad, so the nurse decided to show Lashae the baby and put her crib card on her new crib.

It was 4:30 in the evening, and 'Nasia hadn't heard from RahKe yet. She was still in bed watching TV when she heard Ke's mom say, "That's the wrong room." Ke walked in and gave Ky'Nasia a hug. He told her a song and a dance about why it's twelve hours after his baby was born and she was just getting to see or hear from him. His mom interrupted and asked, "Where's the baby?" The tears began to fall as 'Nasia explained everything to them. His mom asked to speak to the doctor, and she came in and explained everything again. She allowed them to go into the

NICU, but only for a few minutes. 'Nasia let Ke's mom stay in longer. She figured she was going to be there all night, but Ke's mom had to leave. She watched as RahKe and his mother held the baby and checked her out from head to toe. Ke kissed every inch of her, then asked about her not having on any clothes and socks. Going back to the room was hard for 'Nasia after seeing her baby with all those tubes and wires all over her. She cried for a while. RahKe and his mom tried to calm her down, but it was useless. They understood why.

After a few days in the NICU, doctors decided that since Ky'Nasia wasn't breastfeeding the baby and the baby wasn't eating anyway, that they could discharge 'Nasia. She was crushed. She had to leave her baby there while she went home. She cried the entire time they discharged her. She went home that day with thoughts to finish setting up their room. When she got there, her mom and everyone else had gotten her a new bed, dresser, and TV, and almost all of the stuff from the baby shower was put away and hung up. All she had to do was move the bassinet where she wanted it. Not being able to lift or move things for a few weeks, 'Nasia had RahKe put it close to the bed so she could get to it easily.

After resting for about two hours, she was ready to head back to the hospital. RahKe and her mom tried to get her to relax a little longer, but she wanted her baby home. Back at the hospital with her baby girl, she still had tubes everywhere, and she was in a warming house. The nurse let Ky'Nasia know that the doctor was just in with her baby and should be giving her a report soon. The good news was that ZahNyah was gaining weight again, so now they would try to bottle feed her and see how it goes.

The next day, 'Nasia arrived at the hospital, and they told her that her baby girl was on the right track and that ZahNyah may be able to get the tubes removed the next day. They took her off the oxygen when 'Nasia or RahKe was holding her. She was good during the day. Later that night, Ky'Nasia got a call from the hospital saying they had to put her back on oxygen because she dropped in her deep sleep, but there was no cause for concern, her baby girl was fine. They also removed the feeding tube and took her out of the warmer! Her baby girl was doing great. She was eating from a two-ounce bottle without throwing up. She was also holding a steady temperature that was within normal limits. They kept her one more night just to monitor her and to be sure she was ready to go home.

On Wednesday morning, 'Nasia got the call she'd been waiting for, she could finally bring ZahNyah home. All she had to do was come in and be trained on her monitor. Ky'Nasia completed the training, and they were set to go home. They got in the car and headed home. After 'Nasia got in the house, everyone wanted to see the baby. She handed her over to her mom as Ky'Nasia plugged up the monitor. After everyone got a chance to hold the baby, 'Nasia put her down for a nap. It was great to finally have her baby girl home with her. ZahNyah was here to stay!

Round 5

Clinch & Cradle

The joy of her baby girl was short-lived as round five increased her bruising. She learned that RahKe was just like all the rest of the niggas. He had more girls, more partying, and was selling drugs; that was her nightmare, and it all came true. She never wanted her kids to be without their dad, a chance she guessed Ke was willing to take. He did make sure all ZahNyah's needs and wants were well taken care of. They didn't want for anything.

Ky'Nasia had gotten a job at McDonald's as her senior year in high school kicked in. She also had a four-month-old baby girl, was in the color guard, and had a man who was supposed to be in college but was running the streets instead. Graduation time was fast approaching, she had to start looking into colleges. One college had a program that included weekends. She could start now, go to high school Monday through Friday, and then attend college on the weekends. It would allow her to finish her science and engineering degree in two years. Of course, that was a no-go because she had a baby and a job. How was she going to take care of her baby if she was always busy with school and work? The summer ended and 'Nasia didn't have any college plans set in stone and RahKe was still out beating the streets down like nobody's business. It was hard to focus as she watched him become more careless.

At the first home game of the season, ZahNyah and RahKe came to watch the game and see Ky'Nasia perform. Everyone wanted to see her. RahKe, being him, only let a select few hold her. 'Nasia couldn't say much because she understood why Ke was acting like that. She was their prize possession. After 'Nasia was done performing, she came and got the baby. She was such a happy, big baby. Ke made sure nobody was all up on them. Ky'Nasia heard a chick calling Ke name, and they both looked. It was some girl Ke used to talk to back in the day. She was way too excited to see him, so 'Nasia made sure he remembered she was standing there. Ky'Nasia walked a little closer to him, and he noticed the look on her face. RahKe introduced her and the baby to the girl and afterward, she walked off. The game was over, and it was time to go, so RahKe told her he would see her when she got to his mom's house as he and ZahNyah left.

Ky'Nasia caught a ride uptown with her homegirl. She got to Ke's mom's, but he wasn't there. RahKe had put the baby to bed with his mom, so 'Nasia went upstairs and checked on her. His mom said she just went to sleep and for 'Nasia to leave her there, and that she will bring her down when she wakes up. Ky'Nasia headed to the room and made her a bottle. She left it on the table so everyone could see it. She took a shower, then called Ke, but he didn't pick up the phone. Too tired to care, she went to bed.

It's 3:30 am and she felt him grabbing on the covers. "Baby, you hungry? I got some food from Queens."

"Why were you at Queens and why didn't you pick up the

phone when I called you?"

"I was handling some business. The baby is still sleeping. I took her bottle upstairs so they wouldn't have to call down here for it."

"You smell like the liquor store and an ashtray. I thought you were handling business?"

"Not tonight 'Nasia, damn. Do you want some food or no 'cause I am about to eat it?" She sat up and looked at the food. Ke had already eaten most of it. She looked at him crazy and rolled her eyes.

"There's nothing there to eat. This is just the scraps of something you had. So, you went and sat at the diner to eat? Who was there with you?"

"Chill 'Nasia. I just told you I was handling business."

"What the fuck ever! You think somebody dumb. Let me smell you."

"You love to act crazy."

"Goodnight motherfucker, and don't touch me either! Nasty Bitch."

"I should have stayed out. Nobody has time for this bullshit." They went to bed and didn't touch each other.

The next morning, Ky'Nasia got dressed for work and got the baby ready for her day. She was washed, dressed, and had her hair done. 'Nasia made her two bottles and a jar of baby food. She packed her diaper bag and got the stroller ready too. She set it all in the corner of the hallway. 'Nasia came back in the room to let RahKe know where everything was, and Ke damn near jumped out of his skin. Looking at his phone light up, she asked, "Who are you on the phone with this early?"

"Here we go. I can't even be on my phone without being questioned or accused."

"Bye RahKe! Have a great day." That was how his bad behavior started. He was never willing to talk about what was bothering Ky'Nasia. She went to work and worked her shift. It seemed like 4 pm took forever to come. She got home and took a shower. ZahNyah was ready to go outside and play, so 'Nasia took her to the park, and they got on the swings. After being there for over an hour, Ke called her phone, trying to make small talk, and she listened. He asked her where she was and what time was she coming back. 'Nasia continued to play with the baby like she didn't hear him. She headed back to Ke mom's because she knew he was going to come looking for her. Halfway there Ky'Nasia saw RahKe standing on the corner with some girl. 'Nasia walked right between them. RahKe explained to her that she was just buying some bud from him. She didn't believe him as she watched him hand her a balled-up piece of paper. Sick of his bullshit, she walked into the house. It was getting late, so she got ZahNyah ready for bed. Ke came in, finished up, and made her bottles for bed.

They laid down and watched TV until ZahNyah was asleep. Ky'Nasia changed the channel and she followed suit. ZahNyah and Ky'Nasia were passed out by 9 pm. 'Nasia woke up to get the baby a bottle around 1:30 am and Ke was gone. She looked around the entire house and outside, no RahKe anywhere. She called his phone. She could hear girls in the background and asked where he was at. RahKe said, "Here I come. You and the baby were asleep when I left." Over the dumb shit, she packed her stuff to go home the next day. Ke realized that 'Nasia had packed and asked, "Is it that serious?" She just stared at him because he made no sense at all to her.

Then RahKe's phone rings. Ky'Nasia grabbed it. "Hello?"

"Where Dutch? He left his hat at the diner, and I wanted to give it back to him."

"Who is this? And you were at the diner with him the other day?"

"Yeah, who are you? His baby mom?"

"No, I am his girlfriend and his baby mom."

"Oh, well that's not what he said."

"What did he say?" She put the phone on speaker while RahKe was trying to get it out of her hands. The chick told Ky'Nasia how they sometimes meet up at the diner on a late night, have a bite to eat, and maybe even sex, depending on how long it took 'Nasia to realize that Ke was gone. She was heartbroken again. Ky'Nasia hung up the phone and handed it to RahKe. Ky'Nasia grabbed a few blankets and headed to the living room. She set up the couch and put the baby in her bassinet. Tired of the drama she laid down to watch TV. Being King RahKe, he turned the TV off and turned on the lights. Not willing to fight she laid there without the TV. Ke was mad that Ky'Nasia didn't try to turn the TV back on, so he started pulling at the covers. Annoyed, she swung on RahKe. Ke laughed and asked, "You want to fight now?" Pissed she asked him to leave her alone. Not willing to let her be great, he grabbed ZahNyah and took her in the room. Ky'Nasia laid there. Ke called her phone a million times, being smart. 'Nasia heard the baby crying so she came to get her.

RahKe yelled, “No! Get her bottle.” He knew what she wanted. She gave her the bottle. ZahNyah reached for Ky’Nasia, but Ke wouldn’t let her come. ‘Nasia had no choice but to get in bed to stop her baby from crying. ‘Nasia laid down next to her and of course, the minute she fell asleep Ke put her in her bed.

“Let me tell you something. Don’t ever think you will take my baby away from me. Do you hear me? Y’all belong to me. You and her. Y’all are my family! You hear me?!” Ky’Nasia watched RahKe as he pointed his finger in the center of her forehead. His eyes were dark, and his face was wrinkled with anger.

Rolling her eyes, she turned over in bed to face the wall. ‘Nasia felt him get back in bed. RahKe’s dick was so hard. Every time they argued his dick would be hard as a rock. Ky’Nasia pushed herself away from his grip. Ke pulled her closer as his dick forced its way in between her legs. He slid her shorts to the side and pushed his dick inside her. Trying to pull away, he told her to stop fighting it and to look at how wet her pussy had gotten. ‘Nasia couldn’t help how her body responded to him even when she was mad and hurt. She tried her best to act like she wasn’t enjoying it. Ke must have been reading her mind because he started laughing at her. “I know it feels good to you. You better stop biting that lip and let those sounds go, before you don’t have a lip.”

Unable to control herself, she gripped the back of his shirt and enjoyed his manhood. A few soft moans escaped her lips as her body shook with pleasure. RahKe was in her deep and it felt amazing! Her pussy juices dripped down her ass. She could feel the sheets under her getting soaking wet. She entered the world of ecstasy and her orgasm came like the waves of the ocean! Knowing that he was hitting the right spot, Ke lifted her legs up higher on his shoulders. Her pussy opened wider. RahKe bounced around inside her hitting every angle possible. Begging to be fucked Ke told her to get on top. With the look of the devil, Ky'Nasia refused. Hell, she was still mad! Ke understanding that she wasn't beat, he grabbed 'Nasia and flipped her over. Putting her in doggie-style, he went in from the back. Ke started off slow. The strokes were awesome. In and out with the dick tip barely staying in, and then pushing it all the way in slowly. RahKe knew this would drive her crazy and make her beg for more. Sure enough, she did just that. Ky'Nasia pleaded, "Give me my dick." She wanted to feel it. She needed him to fuck that pussy like it was the last time! He grabbed her hips and slammed his dick inside her sweet heaven. She screamed with pleasure. Going faster and harder, they fucked each other for an hour. Ready to explode, RahKe spread her ass cheeks open. With one finger rubbing up and down her ass, her body jerked with pleasure. Sure that his nut was on its way, he gripped her ass tighter and got up off his knees. Knowing he was about to rip her insides, she grabbed the side of the bed. Holding on for dear life, she threw her ass back at him. He fucked her hard and fast, demanding that she give him 'his pussy.' As she begged for mercy, he smacked her ass. "Yeah, I like the way that ass jiggles!" Whack! Whack! It felt so good as she released her nut and he busted too. Hot sex juice dropped out of her pussy as she tried to move. Stuck for a few minutes, she slid to the edge of the bed. Still mad at him, she headed to the bathroom to wash off. RahKe smacked her ass again and said, "Damn! I love that pussy. Don't you give my shit away. I'll kill something for that!" She crawled back into bed and was sleep in a matter of seconds.

The sun came up and Ky'Nasia had to get ready to go home for school the next day. She hated having to leave ZahNyah there and going home to her mom's house. She played with the baby all day. She wanted her dad the minute he walked into the house. She finished getting her stuff together for the week so she wouldn't have to worry about what she would look like when 'Nasia got there from school or work. After getting her stuff ready, Ky'Nasia sat on the front porch and listened to the birds. RahKe came out and let her know he had put the baby down for a nap. He walked off the step saying, "I'll be back before you leave to go to your moms!" Knowing Ke was lying, she went into the house and made dinner.

At school, they were all getting ready for the Holly Ball dance. They couldn't bring any outsider to that event so there was no date for Ky'Nasia! She picked out a short black dress with sparkling blue flowers. She had blue heels and a purse to match. The dance was fun! Almost the entire senior class was there. The teachers crowded the dance floor to make sure there was NO grinding. It was crazy. People were leaving early to go have sex in the parking lot before it was over. After the dance, Ky'Nasia made it to RahKe house. Surprise, surprise. She got there and Ke wasn't home. She called his phone and realized it was in the dresser drawer. Shaking her head, she started going through his phone. All that was in there were a few pictures of them and ZahNyah and a whole bunch of unsaved numbers. 'Nasia got ready for bed. She had to work in the morning.

After work, Ky'Nasia got a shower and took ZahNyah for a walk. There was still no sign of RahKe. As it started to get dark out, 'Nasia and her baby girl headed into the house. Ke pulled up in some car asking if 'Nasia wanted to go get ice cream. She did want ice cream, so she got her and ZahNyah some. Later, they all showered and got ready for bed. The minute they laid down his phone went off. Trying to hurry up and clear the message Ky'Nasia read it first. It read, *'Thanks for coming out last night. I enjoyed myself. Heart eyes.'* She didn't waste her time saying anything 'cause RahKe started to lie before she could even speak.

"My cousin threw a hot ass party last night out in the hood. It was mad people there. That was her just texting me saying thanks for coming." Ky'Nasia just rolled over and went to sleep figuring at least the motherfucker washed his dick before he laid down with her!

Now it was time for 'Nasia to go to Rowan for her EOF interview. She got her baby got ready to go. As she put the stuff in the car, she explained to RahKe where she was going. With a look of surprise, he asked her why she was just telling him about it. Ky'Nasia told him she wasn't sure how he was going to take it. Pissed off, he helped her finish putting the stuff in the car. The people who interviewed Ky'Nasia were very nice. They asked questions about her grades and how she would take care of her baby living on campus. 'Nasia tried to explain to them that she would go home on the weekends and during breaks to take care of ZahNyah. She also explained that her baby girl's dad and grandma would do their part while Ky'Nasia was away at school. Not willing to understand her reasons for wanting to go away to college to get a better career, they denied her. She was heartbroken, so she went to Cumberland County College instead.

Last minute changes caused her to miss out on her senior trip. She couldn't go with her family and to her senior class trip. So, the family vacation won! Ky'Nasia wasn't bothered that she missed her senior class trip until she realized that she wasn't getting her class ring either. Some of the choices she made left her feeling empty. She tried ordering her own ring, but the one she wanted was $675. Her Mom said she would go half with her on a $300 one, but that's not what she wanted. So, no senior trip and no class ring.

Prom was Ky'Nasia next best thing! She couldn't wait for prom! She had her dress made by her older brother's girlfriend. It was jade green, with one shoulder strap, a slit up to her high thigh, and it had rhinestones on it. Ky'Nasia purchased her prom ticket. The night before prom, she got her hair done. She was too cute! 'Nasia got back to the house and she noticed that RahKe had been in her bag. Ke had put her nightgown on the bed for her to put on. Ky'Nasia told him that it was supposed to be worn for something special, and that she didn't want to wear it that night. Not listening to a word she said, Ke pulled the towel off of her and put the nightgown over her head. Putting her arms through the gown, she asked where his suit was for prom. Ke told her he was picking it up in the morning. Ky'Nasia sucked her teeth. RahKe instantly started kissing around her neck and chest. After a few minutes of that, her pussy was throbbing. They went straight to the bed. Having to worry about messing up her hair, she put a hold on a few positions, but the sex was still mind-blowing.

The next day everything for RahKe was last minute, to the point Ky'Nasia cried. She ended up telling her nephew, Flow, that she had to take him with her to prom. 'Nasia ran to the mall to get her jewelry and him some dress shoes. She was really mad. She went home to get dressed and RahKe still didn't have anything to wear. At 'Nasia's mom's house, she showered and got dressed for prom. Her mom took so many pictures, it was crazy! When 6:00 pm came, a limo pulled up in front of her house to pick her up. She asked her mom who sent it and she let her know her brother got it for her. Excited that she had her own limo, she grabbed her purse and other stuff and headed for the door. Just as 'Nasia and Flow finished their ride around the hood, RahKe called to let her know that he was ready. Flow was heated. 'Nasia came and got Ke from his mom's house and they took more pictures there. Happy that she got to take the love of her life to prom with her, she kissed him all over his face.

During prom they danced and took more pictures!

Ky'Nasia had to capture every moment of that day. They ate and made plans to go to Denny's with a few of her friends, but 'Nasia knew she didn't want to do that! Her mind was on fucking! Her boo came through at the very last minute. He didn't leave her hanging! They slowly danced until the lights came on. Her brother paid for the limo until 2 am. They started holding and kissing each other in the limo. RahKe's hands made their way inside the slit of her dress and right to her caramel center. He fingered her for the entire ride home. Once in front of the house, the limo driver asked if they had anywhere else to go or were they done with him for the night. Her pussy was soaking wet so Ky'Nasia told him they were done for the night and thanked him for safely taking them and bringing them home. He gave them all the sodas and water in the limo and told them that they could keep it. They went straight to the bedroom and RahKe unzipped her dress. Her breasts were exposed as it fell to the floor. Like a magnet, his mouth was drawn to them. Sucking on her nipples, 'Nasia rubbed the back of his head. She reached down and grabbed his dick. It was super hard. She tried to pull it through the zipper hole in his pants, but it refused to bend! Stripping naked, Ke laid her on the bed. Pulling out some chocolate syrup and ice cream he asked her, " Can I have fun with your body? Can I turn you into my sundae?"

Horny as hell she nodded her head 'yes'. RahKe took a spoonful of ice cream and rubbed it up and down her stomach. He drizzled chocolate syrup over each one of her breasts and then on to her freshly shaved pussy. RahKe licked from top to bottom as the ice cream slowly began to melt. Ke sucked each nipple and then he put them in his mouth together. His tongue danced around them as he sucked and licked them clean. He paused over top of her as he traced the ice cream down to her pussy with his tongue! A first time for everything! She tried her best to keep her composure. Her body was freaking out! His tongue came up to get more ice cream off of her stomach, then back to heaven he went. Sucking on her clit, he held Ky'Nasia hands and watched her lose her mind. Coming up for more ice cream, he placed each of her legs on his shoulders. He pulled her butt up off the bed and ate her pussy! She begged him to stop. She wasn't sure what was happening to her. Her nuts came back to back like shock waves. She felt like she had died and gone to heaven. She couldn't control it. RahKe asked her if she liked it. She couldn't even catch her breath. Trying to remain calm as he scooped up more ice cream, RahKe turned her over and told her to get on her knees. Ky'Nasia did. Ke placed the scoop of ice cream at the top of her ass. As it ran down her ass, so did his tongue. The ice cream melted into her pussy and he ate that shit from the back. Never in her life was she so scared and excited at the same time. It was a flood in between her legs. She was busting nuts left and right.

Ke asked if she wanted some of 'Big Daddy'. She shook her head yes. He slid him in nice and easy. RahKe took his time with her. Her caramel center was dripping wet. He told her that her pussy tasted good and that he wanted her to nut in his mouth. Stroke after stroke her pussy throbbed. She could feel her nut sliding down her ass. Ke felt her pussy walls getting tight around his dick and he asked her if she was about to nut. Ky'Nasia nodded her head yes as he gave her one last slow stroke before putting his tongue in her heaven. She grinded her pussy to his face with her hands locked around the back of his head. She squirted all in his face and mouth. Not wanting to miss a drop, Ke licked all around her pussy and thighs. She bit her bottom lip as he jammed Kong inside her sweet pussy. Throwing her right leg over his shoulder and placing the left leg in between his, he fucked her so good. She tried to get from under him, but his grip on her shoulders forced her back onto his dick. Kong was hard as a brick and 'Nasia could feel it swelling. Ready to release he grabbed her ass with one hand and pulled on her nipples with the other.

Feeling the nut shoot from his dick, they climaxed together. Hot and heated from the passion, they collapsed.

After a few minutes of rest, Ky'Nasia jumped up and hit the shower. Coming back to bed with a warm soapy washcloth, she cleaned the ice cream and chocolate syrup off his body. RahKe smiled and said, "You always did know how to take care of Daddy."

"I love you!"

"You love me, or you love the way I ate that pussy and fucked you senseless?'

"Both, but I love you more." RahKe wrapped his arms around her as he passed out. With the feeling of love all over her, Ky'Nasia curled up under him and drifted off to sleep. Her night was the best night ever. Her heart was happy at that moment.

Graduation was here and Ky'Nasia was ready to hit the field! Up early, she went to the nail salon. Her nails and feet were on fleek, LA Nails did an awesome job. Then she went straight to the mall to grab her an outfit to wear under her cap and gown. Hitting a few spots, she pieced together her outfit to match her nails and feet perfectly. Leaving the mall with a complete outfit and shoes included, she went to the hair salon to get her hair done. She got a fresh blowout. Her hair was poppin' and flowing. She wrapped her hair up in a scarf so it would still be nice for graduation. Now 'Nasia could relax until it was time to go.

After shaving her legs, underarms, and pussy, she hopped in the shower. The water had to be cold and the bathroom had to be door open to avoid the stream getting to her hair. She laid across the bed for a few minutes to air dry and then she got dressed. She combed her hair down and headed to graduation.

They lined up to get ready in the gym and started to walk to the field. Her family came just in time to take pictures before they walked over. Baby girl and RahKe were right there in every photo. Proud of 'Nasia, Ke kissed her forehead and went to his seat. The class of 2004 hit the field strong. They were proud to finish high school and move on to the next chapter in life. Some of them started college the very next month and that included Ky'Nasia. She was going to be a CCC student on July 2nd. Getting to her seat, she sat there and waited for her name to be called. Of course, she was in the front row because she was short! 'Nasia looked through the crowd until she spotted RahKe, her mom, and baby girl. She saw them waving at her like mindless idiots, so she waved back and smiled. Moments like this made it all worth it. She got up to walk across the stage and the tears began to fall. She was so happy she made it. She did this with a baby on her hip. Ky'Nasia did it. Finally reaching the stage, she got ready to get her diploma. She stepped up onto the stage and heard everyone going crazy. Ky'Nasia looked up and RahKe was holding their baby girl up in the air. 'Nasia danced across the stage shaking the hand of the principal. As she grabbed her diploma, she froze for a photo. Everything around her went blank. She could see everything and everyone, but there was no sound. Her life flashed before her and she knew that was it. She was a young adult with a baby to provide for. As the sound slowly returned, Ky'Nasia continued dancing off the stage. She paused a few more times for more pictures on the way to her seat. Excited to have that part of her life over, the class of 2004 threw their caps in the air after the moving of the tassel. Ky'Nasia was so happy that she could say she was her mom's only girl to walk across the field. She couldn't believe it.

High school was over, and she completed what everyone told her she wouldn't. She even signed up and was going to college. Ky'Nasia was unstoppable. Nothing could take the smile off her face at that point. At project graduation, 'Nasia and her friends had so much fun. They ripped and ran all over that place. They had games, food, face painting, and so much to do that night. On the bus ride home, Ky'Nasia called RahKe to let him know she was on her way there and to have the door unlocked. She made it back to the school and her mom dropped her off to Ke's house.

She walked into the kitchen and the table was set up with balloons and things that Ky'Nasia liked to eat. There was fruit, crabs, and chocolate. Smiling from ear to ear, RahKe walked up to her and handed her a card. Ke kissed her forehead and then her lips. He told her congratulations as he led her to the bedroom. The room was lit with candles and the camera was set up by the bed. RahKe asked did she want to eat some of her stuff or put it away for tomorrow. They put everything away except the chocolate. That was needed in the bedroom. After showering, she headed to the bedroom and watched him get undressed. Sitting on the edge of the bed, he pulled her into him. They started kissing as his hands rubbed the back of her neck, legs, ass, and around to her throat. Asking her if it is ok to record this one, she nodded yes. Reaching over, RahKe turned on the video camera and it was lights, camera, action. He slid his hand down her neck to her breast as the towel hit the floor. While sucking and rubbing on her breast, Ke fed her a chocolate covered strawberry. RahKe bit it and then seductively pushed it into his mouth. Sucking on her breast he worked his fingers down to her caramel square. He ran his fingers across her clit and she almost dropped to the floor. Feeling her body getting weak, Ke laid her across the bed. He leaned forward and asked her if he could do what he wanted to her beautiful body. Hot and bothered she agreed. That grin spread across his face like wildfire. She was hooked. She wouldn't stop him if he tried to tie her to a train.

RahKe grabbed the strawberries and they shared one with a

kiss. Ready to get the show on the road, he poured champagne on her belly. Starting from her breasts, he licked it all up. Most of it was in her belly button. The chills that ran down her spine had her body shaking. Ke laughed as he watched her body hit a new high. Spreading her legs open, Ke pulled her to the edge of the bed so her ass was hanging off. He twisted her hips up in the air and poured the champagne inside her heaven. He stuck his tongue, which had a small piece of strawberry on it, in her pussy. Flicking his tongue around made her arch her back. That was different. He sucked the champagne out of her pussy as he continued to eat her caramel square. Being sure he got it all, he flexed her hips down and let the rest drip into his mouth. It drove her crazy. Ke played with her clit with his tongue, then he asked if she was ready. Ky'Nasia wanted more of whatever he was about to give her, so she said yeah.

With that being said, he grabbed the oil from the nightstand. Ke flipped her over onto her stomach. The oil hit the middle of her back and he began to massage her back. Rubbing her body from head to toe, he didn't miss a beat. He poured a little champagne down the crack of her ass and licked it off. Opening her ass and kissing it, he let her ass cheeks hit his face and sucked all around the outside of her cheeks. He smacked it as he ran his hand over the crack of her ass. Ke slid his fingers in her ass and Ky'Nasia let out a squeal. Wow! That was definitely different. He ran his other hand across the top of her ass as he slowly eased his finger into her ass. It was painful at first, but he made sure not to hurt her. He leaned in to check on her and kissed her neck. Ky'Nasia's body didn't know what to do. The crazy thing is, she wanted more of it. While fingering her ass, he played with her pussy. His dick brushed up against her leg, and it was super hard! She felt the precum dripping from his dick. Feeling her excitement, he slid his dick in her pussy. He stroked her slowly because his fingers were still in her ass and she melted. Enjoying it, she winded her hips. Her release was crazy, and nut poured out of her pussy. Feeling it down his legs, he asked if she'd liked that. Freaking out, she screamed, "Yes."

"Tell me my dick good."

"Daddy this dick is great, but you gotta slow down 'cause it's too deep."

"How deep is it?"

"It's touching my throat. It feels like it's ripping my insides." She pushed him back a little to give her pussy some relief. Knowing what Ky'Nasia was trying to do, RahKe eased her up on the bed. Laying her flat on her stomach, he put the condom on and mounted her ass. He lubed the condom up with juices from her pussy, and gently put it in her ass. Ke took his time with it and told her to relax. He asked if it hurt and if she wanted him to stop. Not sure how she felt at that moment, she said, "Just do it soft and go really slow." Understanding that it hurt like hell, Ke slowed down even more and only put the head in. Doing that a few times allowed her body to adjust and she fiend for more. He slowly lifted her ass off the bed and pushed his dick in a little further.

"Yeah, you like that shit now. It feels good to you now. Tell me you want this dick. Look at how your ass shakes. Fuck. This shit feels amazing. Damn, I love this pussy. I love you, girl." Smiling, he wiped sweat from his face and neck as he pushed inside her a little deeper. Moans escaped her lips as she held on for dear life. With each stroke and stride, he went deeper and faster. Hearing his breathing change, she knew he was about to nut. He tapped her on her ass and said," Get on your knees."

She did as she was told. RahKe slid his dick back into her ass. His hand was fingering her sweet pussy and clit. The pain was very minimal as he continued to fuck her ass. Feeling more and more pleasure, she started to throw it back at him. "Hell yeah baby! Take this dick! Can I fuck you?" Pulling on her shoulders his entire dick entered her. Speechless, her face hit the bed which caused her ass to tut up higher. That allowed him to go even deeper. Grabbing the pillows and covering her screams, she tried her best to take all of his dick! She couldn't handle it. She finally was able to push him back and control his strokes. Not wanting her to be in pain or uncomfortable, he pulled out. Turning her over, he removed the condom. She mounted him in the sixty-nine position, sucking his balls and dick as he ate her pussy and ass. Ky'Nasia could feel her pussy swelling in his mouth as he sucked the nut out of her. She could taste his precum. She licked his dick clean. His dick was so big, it gagged her a few times. She sucked his dick as if it was a piece of ice on a burning hot summer day. She got off his face so she could watch his face as she sucked the life out of him. She spit on his dick and sucked the soul out of his body. Watching as his toes curled and his hands grabbed the sheets, she sucked harder. She licked his balls and went back up for more. Knowing he was damn near on edge and about to bust, she sucked his dick and allowed it to gag her a few more times before relaxing her throat and allowing his dick to dance with her tonsils. Her hands weren't exempted. They worked the portion of his dick that couldn't fit in her mouth. She felt his nut building up, so she sucked his entire dick. She had his whole dick in her mouth. He went crazy. He started fucking her mouth. She held his dick in there and continued to suck it. Grabbing the back of her head and tightening up his legs, he yells, "Oh Shit! Fuck 'Nasia! Damn, wait a minute." Ke dick swelled up in her mouth. Sucking and slobbering, she got more into the groove. She felt the first shot of cum. She sucked faster and harder as his nut shot deep in the back of her throat. 'Nasia swallowed it all. "Shit, 'Nasia. How did you do me like that? I thought you didn't like sucking dick."

"Just because I don't like doing it doesn't mean I don't know how or can't please you by doing it. I take care of business. Shit, we both tried something new."

Cleaning each other off, RahKe stopped the video. He took the tape out of the camera and handed it to Ky'Nasia. He told her to never give it to anyone and that it was hers to keep. She put the tape away and changed the sheets. Climbing in the bed, they both were dead. That took a lot out of them and they were asleep in a matter of seconds. Hearing a knock at the door, they woke up. "Your daughter wants her Dad." Putting on his clothes, he went to the door and got her. "Good job mommy," she said as she got in the bed with them and went to sleep. Before dozing off, 'Nasia reflected on her entire day. Graduation night was a success. Ky'Nasia had her whole family there to support her including her man and princess.

Round 6

Blow by Blow

Starry eyed, 'Nasia got up for round six which came in strong, knocking her flat on her ass. Life as they knew it was changing. RahKe was in the streets heavy! His new life was all about selling drugs, having guns, and being in the spotlight. 'Nasia was in her second year of college, and ZahNyah was two years old now. 'Nasia was working at Ancora, a psychiatric hospital, making good money. One night, after picking her up from class they had to ride to Brotmanville, NJ. Ke hopped out of the car to talk with his boys. She knew something was wrong because he jumped in the car and rushed home. She asked if everything was okay and Ke said, "Yes. Nothing for you to worry about." 'Nasia knew better because his nose was sweating and his face was twisted. Getting out of the shower she checked on Sweet Pea. She was fast asleep. Ky'Nasia walked into the bedroom, but Ke was gone. She texted his phone, and he hit back instantly, *"I'll be home in an hour. I had to bust a move real quick. I love you."* Not knowing what to think, she got in bed and watched TV until she dozed off.

The next morning 'Nasia headed to work like she normally

did, but Ke asked if she could leave work early. Not sure why, she said she'd be home after lunch. "Nasia got home and Ke was on the step talking to Shatek. Ky'Nasia walked up to him and asked why he needed her to come home early. RahKe explained that he needed to go somewhere, but it had to wait a little while because his boy was at work. Looking at the bitch still standing there, 'Nasia asked if she could help her. Rolling her eyes, Shatek waved bye and stepped off. The argument was on. "Why was she comfortable enough to stand there while we talked? Are you fucking her again? Am I supposed to be okay with you hanging with a bitch I know you fucked? Nigga, you're buggin'."

"Come on 'Nasia. Why is that the first thing out of your mouth? I do have some type of respect for you and me. She was smoking a blunt with me. We literally just finished it! I ain't fucking that girl. That's done."

"Whatever you say!" She called her niece, Olivia, and they went to get an outfit from the mall. Later that night, they headed to the bar down the street and had a few drinks. 'Nasia listened to the jukebox and played a game of pool. Ke's boy was there, so she knew it wouldn't be long before he would show his face. Sipping on her Sex on the Beach, she grooved to the music. Musiq Soulchild's song *Love* came on when Ky'Nasia felt a tap on her shoulder. She turned around and saw her old classmate, Malachi. He bought her a drink, and they talked for a bit. She felt herself getting tired, so she headed for the door, and let Olivia know she was out. Olivia said she was staying with Ke's boy Roc and he would get her home. As 'Nasia was leaving, she saw Ke walking up to the door. RahKe asked 'Nasia if she was ready to go home now or if they were having another drink. Laughing at how crazy his ass was, she pushed passed him because she didn't have it in her to argue in public. Straight to the house and to bed they went.

Days later, a detective showed up asking questions about Ke's whereabouts on a particular night in question. 'Nasia told them he was home watching football with her. Weeks go by and she asked Ke why the cops were asking her questions. Of course, RahKe did his best keeping 'Nasia out of his bullshit. That was one of the things Ky'Nasia loved about him. RahKe always protected home. Telling her as little as possible, they kept it moving. October hit and shit went left. The DT's were constantly riding by the house and pulling up watching their every move. They stayed in the house for the night, sat down and had dinner.

After the game went off, they headed to the bed to finish what they'd started. Pulling her pants off her hips, he gently kissed her neck. Getting the pants down to her ankles, he pushed her legs into the frog position. RahKe placed one finger in his mouth and then on her clit. Rubbing it slow and firm with pressure, he sucked on her nipples. Sliding one finger into her sweet box, her juices flooded his hand. That grin crept across his face. Kong was rock hard as it slid over her leg and in her pussy. Fucking her slow, he asked, "Promise me you will never leave me no matter what!" In the heat of the moment, 'Nasia promised him – not even sure of why or what she was promising. Feeling something different about that night, she watched his face and body language as he worshipped her body. He touched her in ways he'd never done before and sucked on every one of her toes, one at a time. RahKe licked every inch of her, all in slow motion. He did it as if he was taking mental notes and photos of every inch of her body. That shit was amazing! She was busting nuts just from his touch! This night was different. It felt like Ke wanted her more than ever. Pulling her up and off of the bed, he told her, "Ride Daddy slow. Take your time. I want it to last a long time. I want us to enjoy each other." Thinking to herself, 'Okay, I'll try to compose myself,' she climbed on top, put his tip in and slid down slowly. That shit right there drove 'Nasia crazy. She winded her hips gently and easily, taking the dick in and out of her pussy. As the tip of his dick hit the front of her pussy, she gripped it tighter and moved down it slowly. She forced herself to control her nut as she was losing her mind. She spun around while sitting on his dick, she wanted some of that action cowgirl style. Grabbing her ass, he told her, "Go slow! I want to watch this dick invade that pussy."

Going slow they fucked cowgirl style. Ke pushed up into her and pulled his legs from under her. They ended up doing it doggie-style, his favorite position. Kissing all over her ass, he entered her from behind.

"Promise you will never give my pussy away. Tell Daddy this is his pussy."

Doing just that she said, "I promise this is your pussy Daddy! This dick is so good. I promise not to give your pussy away." With that being said, Ke went fucking nuts. He grabbed her ass so hard and fucked the shit out of her. Pounding that pussy, she screamed in pleasure and in pain. "Damn Daddy, what's wrong? Why are you fucking me like this? Slow down. You're being rough." Trying to push him back a little and slow him down, he grabbed her and went even harder. There was no escape. Feeling his dick expanding inside her sweet box, she braced herself.

"Give me my pussy! I need to know who shit this is!"

"Baby, please!"

"No, tell me. I know you feel that dick swelling up."

"Please, slow down!"

"I'm about to nut. Shake that ass on my dick." Smack! Her ass jiggled. Smack! Smack!

"Yeah, that's the shit I like. Look at that ass jiggle." Smack! "Fuck that shit feels so good. I love this pussy!" With one last stroke, he fell right on top of her. Not able to move, they laid there breathing heavily. She reached over to get his hand. She asked, "Is everything okay?" The look in his eyes let her know that only time would tell.

"Just promise me that no matter what, you will always have my back. You're never gonna leave me out to dry. I love you, and I need you. You and ZahNyah are all I got!"

Hearing the seriousness in RahKe's voice, she kissed his face and cuddled up next to him. "You will always have me no matter what. We're in this together. Just love me. I love you too." They fell asleep ass naked in each other's arms.

October 5, 2005, 'Nasia was hit with a strong blow as the door got kicked in. Lights were flashing and cops were everywhere. Ky'Nasia grabbed her shirt as the officers pointed their guns at them. ZahNyah was in the bed crying. She watched helplessly as they threw RahKe to the floor. Confused as to why they were being so extra, she asked if she could put her clothes on. They watched as 'Nasia grabbed her stuff off of the floor and quickly dressed. Their guns were still drawn and pointed. Walking them out into the living room, they cuffed RahKe. Tears fell from Ky'Nasia's eyes as she remembered the conversation they had last night. He was arrested and faced life in prison. Damn, took another hit. She felt like her world was over. She sat at the police station while they prepared to interrogate her about stuff she honestly didn't know about. They held her there for hours. Finally, able to go, she asked if she could see RahKe, but they told her no. They said he was being charged with felony murder! Her heart hit the floor as all the air left her body. This couldn't be real. Her baby was too young.

RahKe was locked up on a $250,000 bail and they offered him thirty years in prison. Wow. After they released 'Nasia, she went home and started making phone calls. After three long days of collecting money, signatures, and paperwork, they were still $2,000 short of his bail. She called Ke's other uncle, P Mac, and he gave $1,000. 'Nasia put up $750 and Ke's cousin did the rest. Stressed to the max, she waited for his release. The day Ke came home they looked for a place to live and a lawyer for his case.

On November 14th, they moved into their own place on the south side. Leaving his mom's house was easy. They picked up everything that was theirs and set the house up in one day. It was close to Thanksgiving, so they went food shopping and got ready for the holiday. The night before Thanksgiving, Ky'Nasia cooked most of the food and put the turkey in the oven. She got in bed at 2:30 am. They slept in each other's arms until she got up at 7 am to finish cooking. When all the food was done, they got dressed and headed to the game.

The Thanksgiving Day game featured Millville versus Vineland. They walked around and chatted with everyone they knew. Millville won! They hurried back home to have dinner. RahKe dropped her off and went to his mom's house while 'Nasia warmed up the food. She called him when everything was done, but He didn't pick up the phone. She called his mom and she said that he left ZahNyah there and was gone. She tried calling again. No results, so she shot him a text. She made her plate and went into the room to eat alone. She was on edge, but she hung in there because God knew her heart, and He was not going to do her like that.

RahKe walked through the door at 7:25 pm. "Baby, I am sorry it took so long. I had to bust a few moves and then I was at my mom's house. I only ate a little bit over there so I could eat with you."

Ky'Nasia sat in the bedroom as tears rolled down her face. "You are facing thirty years in prison. This is our first Thanksgiving together in our own place, and I spent it alone. I ate dinner alone. Then, when you finally show your face, you are super drunk and high out of your mind. I know you weren't at your mom's this long. I've been calling both of y'all all day. You're the only one who didn't pick up. Why didn't you pick up?"

"Why do I have to deal with this bullshit? I am the only one facing life in prison. When I am behind the wall, you will be free to do what you want. Let me fucking live. Shit. Yeah, I had a few drinks and smoked some weed. I need to relax my mind."

"You know what? Fuck it. I will be straight." She started packing up the food and putting it away. She finished cleaning off the table and hopped in the shower. Ke was sitting in the hallway on the phone. Then he walked to the corner. After the shower, 'Nasia got dressed and went to the bar. Ke was on her heels trying to talk, but she wasn't feeling him at that moment. Sitting at the bar listening to Jagged Edge's song *Promise,* Ke stood next to her singing. It felt so real and believable, but she knew it was all part of his game. She ducked and dodged, and tried her best not to feed into his mess. Ke pulled her off the stool towards the dance floor. He sang in her ear with everything in him. He whispered, "I can't lose you now. I need you now more than ever. Please forgive me for being selfish. I love you and I never meant to hurt you." The promises and apologies all sounded the same. They danced until the song was over. Ke walked her to the car, and they headed home.

The ride to the house was filled with mixed emotions and conversation. Ke tried to explain, "I have a lot on my mind and I just need to be out for a little bit without seeing the look of disappointment on your face. When I look at you all I see is hurt and pain. You smiled so beautifully this morning. I wanted to keep that vision in my head for as long as possible. I feel like I failed you and ZahNyah. I have to go do time and I don't even have a clue as to how long or even when I am going to trial. This shit got crazy real fast. I am just trying to figure out how I can make sure y'all good while I am gone. I love y'all more than anything in this world."

"I get that you have a lot to deal with and think about, but that doesn't give you the right to disregard my feelings. I am going through it too. I am just going to be out here alone." She grabbed her keys and went into the house. Ke followed and got in the shower, but his phone started to ring, and it continued ringing. 'Naisa was tired of it ringing, so she looked at it. The text read, *"I know you just left me, but I wish you could've stayed a little longer. I really could use a cuddle buddy."* Another blow to hurt 'Nasia, but curiously, she checked his voicemail. *'Hey Ke. I wish you would stop by soon. I really miss your presence. I need to see your face. Call me when you can.'* She sent the voicemail to her phone and took a screenshot of the texts. She turned the phone on silent and went to bed.

Ke entered the room and wanted to talk, but 'Nasia was in her feelings and it showed. Ke wrapped his arms around her and said he was sorry a thousand times. He cuddled up close and kissed her neck. "I just want to give y'all the world and make sure y'all are safe in it." He pushed her over on her back. Lifting the covers off her body, he spread her legs open and feasted on her sweet heaven. Her nectar flooded into his mouth. He sucked and licked her pussy until his mouth was numb. He came up for air after what felt like forever. Her legs and body shook like crazy as her body came down off a high she couldn't explain. They laid in bed, wrapped in each other's arms.

The morning dawned and it was time to put up the tree. Ky'Nasia and ZahNyah were waiting for Ke to get back from the store. The corner of the living room was cleaned out and ready for the tree. Ke came back with the tree and decorations and set it on the living room floor and asked 'Nasia to come in the room. "Can we put the tree up after the parade because I need to bust a move really quick."

"You know we put the tree up early in the day. It's already 4:30 pm. The parade starts at 7 pm." She was so pissed and frustrated, she walked out. "We will just do it without you. We might as well start doing things without you 'cause the way things are looking, you're too busy for us." She wiped her tears away and opened the tree. ZahNyah and 'Nasia began putting the tree together as Ke leaned up against the wall and watched for a minute. Ke joined in and helped spread the branches apart. "This is how someone legs were last night, he said under his breath." Plucking his ear 'Nasia said, "Shut up. That ain't something she needs to hear about," talking about ZahNyah. Smiling he rubbed the back of his ear and smacked her ass. She turned around and bit down on her bottom lip.

Before the parade, they had leftover Thanksgiving dinner at the table like a family. They finished decorating the tree and went to the parade. They parked their car early and got great seats. They ate cotton candy and ZahNyah begged her Dad to buy her a light up toy. It was twenty-four dollars. Of course, he bought one for her. She played with it until it died. When it was time to go, everyone was ready except Ke. Like always, he managed to step off and was nowhere to be found. She called his phone twice and got no response. They got into the car and went to the house. Ke wasn't there either. 'Nasia texted him, *"Where are you? Are you ok? You left without saying anything. Let me know if you are good."*

She got herself and the baby ready for bed. She stayed in the shower until the water got cold and her skin was wrinkled. After a nice shave and shower, she curled up in bed with her mini me. That was something she was gonna have to get used to, it just being the two of them. Time wasn't on their side.

At 3:15 am, Ky'Nasia hears ZahNyah talking to a man, so she grabbed the bat and headed quietly into the living room. Once she was able to see who it was, she put the bat down. "When did you get here? And why are you up out of bed little girl?"

"I got here about thirty minutes ago. She's up talking to her Dad. Is that a crime?"

"No, but I want to know where she is at all times. That scared me. You almost got your fucking head knocked off." She used the bathroom and then went back to bed. Ke comes in the room, "Is it ok if I get in the bed? Or is the couch my best friend? You know I don't know how many nights I will be able to sleep with you."

"Do us both a favor and stop using that shit as a ticket to do what you want. It's getting old and fast. If the streets are what you want, then be there. Don't just use me pretending that I'm your support system." The bed felt cold that night even though Ke was in it. He kept his distance from her. It was like she knew he had done something wrong, again.

Morning came and the police were at the door again. RahKe had stolen some girl's credit cards and phone. She told the police that he wasn't there and that she hadn't seen him since the parade.

"You know if he gets in any more trouble he can kiss his

bail goodbye," the police officer said with a smile on his face.

Ky'Nasia nodded her head as she shut the door. It was a reality check for her ass. Her man was out on a $250,000 bail, he's cheating on her, and he had the cops looking for him over some dumb shit. That nigga was facing life in prison and he's out there fucking around with that hoe. Ke came to the door to make sure the cops were gone. 'Nasia grabbed the keys and left Ke and ZahNyah in the house.

Round 7

A Special Contender

Like lightning, round seven hit her as she was busy catching up with life as a teenage mother. Ky'Nasia tried her best to stay close to RahKe, but he pulled away even more. There were many times when she crawled into an empty bed, and plenty more when they laid next to each other, never touching or saying a word to one another. It was weird, but that behavior continued for weeks.

One night, RahKe came in around ten o'clock. He was on the phone laughing and grinning. 'Nasia asked him if he was ready to eat, and he looked up at her like she was interrupting something, so she headed up the stairs to check on ZahNyah. Ky'Nasia heard him say, "Yeah, I am in for the night 'cause she's about to be on her bullshit. I will come through when she leaves for work in the morning." Ke hung up the phone and headed right to the bedroom.

After getting Sweet Pea fed and ready for bed, Ky'Nasia went to bed after showering. She never got in the bed without a shower. He asked, "So I can't get nothing to eat? Why'd you run and take a shower? Ain't shit been happening in this bed, and it ain't about to start 'cause you took a shower!"

"Nigga what are you talking about? You know I take a shower every night! This ain't nothing new. You're buggin!" She walked to the kitchen and warmed up his plate and brought it back to the room.

"And don't ever try to play me like I am dirty, or I stink. You're crazy as hell. You know I shower at least twice a day, if not more. If you don't want to have sex with me that's fine, but don't make it seem like it's 'cause I ain't clean."

Eating his plate, he looked at her like she was poisonous; as if she was going to do something to him. She tried to remain calm, so she drank a glass of wine. Ke continued to stare at her like she was crazy. Fully dressed he took his shoes off and got in the bed. Normally he would at least change his clothes before he got in bed, but tonight was different. RahKe kept everything on. She watched in total shock. He grabbed the covers and threw them over his body. When Ky'Nasia tried to get some, he tucked it under his body. Knowing that she didn't want to fight, she got a sheet from the closet. It was cold back there with just a sheet, but she toughed it out.

In the middle of the night, 'Nasia got up to use the bathroom and noticed Ke was gone. Another disappearing act, she thought to herself, but when she came out of the bathroom he was coming back into the room. Ke was high as a kite. He went out to have a smoke. He put his phone on the charger and went to sleep. 'Nasia got his phone and started reading the text messages to see who he was talking to that day. She hit the most recent text and it read, *"I can't wait until morning to see you. Come smoke an L with me. I will be on your porch at 1:30 am. Please don't leave me hanging."* 'Nasia was surprised and hurt, all in the same breath. The number had no name, so she just called it to see who would pick up. "Hey baby, you miss me already? I just left."

"What's your name?" Dial tone. She had hung up on Ky'Nasia. 'Nasia tapped Ke on the shoulder. "Yo, who's the chick you was just smoking with?"

"Why the fuck are you going through my phone? Are you crazy?"

"Who is she and how long have you been dealing with her? We ain't had sex in 3 weeks, so are you fucking her?"

"You're the one who is always so tired then goes right to sleep!"

"You come in at 3 am, and I have to get up at 5 am for work! I try to wake you up before I go to work, and you snap on me."

"'Cause by then I am sleeping and don't want it anymore. I am tired too."

"So, go fuck and be with another bitch?"

"You said it not me."

"Wow. Okay. I see how this will go."

'Nasia grabbed her shit for work and headed to the living room. She heard him yell, "And fuck you too. I don't want that shit anyway."

Ky'Nasia heart was broken. She felt as lonely as ever. She laid on the couch until her alarm for work went off. She hit the shower, got ZahNyah ready, and headed out the door to work. At work, she couldn't help but think about RahKe's plan to meet up while she was gone. She couldn't function. She did her work in a hurry. Lunchtime came and she called to check on baby girl. RahKe answered the phone with an attitude. He told Ky'Nasia how their princess's day went and that she was sleeping. Ky'Nasia looked at the time and told him not to let her nap for too long or she wouldn't go to bed on time. Ke paid her no attention and hung up the phone.

After work, she came home to an empty house. She checked upstairs and no one was there. Her phone rang as she hit the last step. "The kids are across the street at Unc's house. I had to make a run real quick. I will be home in a bit."

Ky'Nasia got the kids and fed them. Of course, ZahNyah was looking for her dad. 'Nasia was told that they were over there all day, and ZahNyah was hungry. She tried not to let that stress her, but it was already taking a toll on her. She waited patiently for Ke to get back. He never made it, so she made dinner and watched TV until she got sleepy. They took their showers and got ready for bed. As dark was approaching, she heard the phone ring. She picked up and it was Ke's friend telling her that Ke got pulled over and the boys were searching the car. She asked where Ke was, and J-Money said they were taking Ke to the county jail. He had a warrant, and it was $750. She rolled her eyes because she knew it was going to be up to her to get him out. When she got to the police station they tried to pretend that they didn't know what she was talking about. An hour later, RahKe walked into the office. Surprised to see her there Ke dropped his head and said, "Thank you."

She asked about the car and where it was parked. RahKe's mom took her to get the car. Later on, he still was unwilling to explain or talk about it and he went to bed. Tears filled her eyes as she looked at his 'fuck you' expression as he curled up and went to sleep. It was late and she had to work in the morning, so she went to bed. RahKe's phone buzzed all night. She wanted to check it so bad but decided it was best not to touch it. She got up and turned it off.

The weekend came and 'Nasia was off. One of Ky'Nasia's guy friends, Malachi, from high school ran into her at the gas station. It was innocent. They texted and called each other a few times throughout the weekend. She ended up running into Malachi again at the mall that Monday. He asked if they could have lunch together. Ky'Nasia told him she would let him know. She got home and Ke was walking down the street with that hoe Shatek again. Not beat for the bullshit 'Nasia went in the house to put her shit away. RahKe came in talking shit as usual. "Why the fuck is your face always twisted up? I am out here trying to get this fucking money to pay these fucking bills. Why you gotta be so damn sensitive? I can't even make a fucking move with you catching a fucking attitude. This shit's annoying. What, you on your period?"

As Ke continued to talk shit, Ky'Nasia phone buzzed in her pocket. She texted Malachi back and let him know that now wasn't a good time to talk. Ke noticed a smile on her face and asked, "Is that your new nigga? He got that ass smiling. I ain't seen that shit in a while. Tell that nigga he will die fucking with what's mine! I will kill both of y'all. You hear me Ky'Nasia?"

"Boy, fuck you and everything you're talking about! You crawl out of bed with me in the middle of the night to go be with your bitch! Why do you care who or what puts a smile on this face? You don't even like looking at it. I thought you were my man, but that's clearly wrong!"

"You heard what the fuck I said! You better tell that nigga

to keep it fucking moving."

Walking to the bathroom, he slammed the door. She could hear him moving around in there as she got dinner ready for the night. She cooked white rice, corn on the cob, and fried chicken. She made plates and put his in the microwave. After everyone had eaten, Ky'Nasia cleaned the kitchen and got ZahNyah ready for bed. RahKe came into the bathroom and kissed them both.

"I will be back after I get rid of all this shit," he said showing her the crack he held in the palm of his hand. "'Nasia, you know I love you. I am just trying to do my best to take care of y'all. You and ZahNyah are all I got. Y'all are my family and I am responsible for y'all. Please just let me do what I do. I promise I am going to make sure y'all good. I need you. You're my Queen. You got to chill and stop being so jealous." Ke kissed her forehead.

"Wait Daddy. I want to go with you," ZahNyah said. He kissed her and told her he would be back.

Everything was finished and Ky'Nasia was beat. She hit the shower and went to bed. Before her eyes closed she received a text from Malachi, *"Goodnight beautiful. I hope you sleep well."* A smile spread across her face. She hadn't received a text like that in months. 'Nasia texted back, *"Thanks. You do the same."*

"Don't forget to let me know when we can have lunch. I would love to catch up with you. It's been a minute."

"I will let you know. I work and my days off vary. It would be nice to catch up with you too."

"Okay. Goodnight."

"Goodnight."

It was one o'clock in the morning and she heard the door slam shut. She jumped up out her sleep and grabbed the bat. Staying in the room with the bat ready to go she waits as RahKe comes into the room. "Ky'Nasia, it's me. I am home babe. I am a little drunk, but I made it."

He fell onto the bed. She turned on the light to see what was going on. Ke laid there with his eyes closed. "I'm hungry babe. Can you get my plate? And bring me something to drink? My mouth is dry. I need a big cup too." Warming up his plate she could hear him singing the Boyz 2 Men song, *I'll Make Love to You*. 'Nasia knew what that meant. Shaking her head, she headed back to the bedroom with the plate and juice. Ke told her to sit the plate on the dresser and to give him the juice. He drank the whole cup and asked for more juice. When she returned to the room, he was in bed. She turned out the light and got in the bed. Before reaching her spot at the back of the bed, Ke asked her, "Do you love me?'

"Yes. You know I love you! I don't love how you treat me."

"Come let me show you how much I love you. Come sit on Daddy's face." Confused as to why Ke requested that, she asked, "Are you sure?"

"Sit on Daddy's face. I want to taste what's mine. It's mine, right?"

"Yes," she said as she climbed on his face. Feeling his tongue hit her clit, her pussy instantly got wet. Ke licked and sucked her caramel square as she rode his face. Flipping her over onto her back he ate the box like it was his last supper. Ke switched into the sixty-nine position as he slowly fucked her mouth. Nut splashed all over his face. He sucked it all up. He asked her if she could swallow his nut. Sucking his dick harder and faster, he exploded in her mouth. Ke grabbed her up from the foot of the bed and planted kisses all over her body. “Damn girl, I love you. Can I hold you?”

Snuggling in close, they went to bed in each other’s arms naked. The bed was warm that night. She didn’t sleep alone, and he had touched her in places she hadn’t been touched in weeks. She felt bad because she knew it wouldn’t last.

The morning was near, and she had to work. Her alarm went off, and she was still in Ke’s arms.

“Babe, call out. I want us to spend the day together.”

“Okay, I will.”

After calling out sick from work, she laid back down. RahKe wrapped her arms around him, and they fell back to sleep. They laid in bed most of the morning until Ke got up and made breakfast. They ate breakfast in bed and watched *National Security*. Then, Ke told her he had to go get something from his boy J-Money. He grabbed a bag from behind the door and told her to get dressed. “Be ready by the time I get back. I am spending the day with my Queens and my night with my Queen! We’re about to paint the city blue. Y’all clothes are in the bag behind the bed.” Ke leaned in and kissed her on the forehead before hurrying out the door.

‘Nasia showered and got ZahNyah ready to go. As they were dressed and waiting for Ke, they watched cartoons and played I spy. ZahNyah was getting restless while waiting to see her dad so she made Ky’Nasia call him.

“Dad, I want you. Come get me.”

"Daddy's coming. Give me a few minutes."

"Okay, but hurry up."

"I love you, Balded Bean."

"I love you too. Mom, dad is on his way in a few minutes. Put my shoes on. I am going with my dad."

"Okay little girl. Go get your shoes," said 'Nasia. While cleaning up the kitchen, a knock on the door startled her. Walking to the window she peeked out to see who it was. It was Shatek. She was banging on the door like a crazy person. 'Nasia open the door and Shatek almost fell in. "Can I help you?" Ky'Nasia's attitude was on a hundred!

"Yes, is Ke here?"

"Girl, what the fuck is wrong with you?"

"I just wanted to get some weed from him. He's not picking up the phone."

"He must not want to talk. Get off my step."

Ke pulls up and jumps out of the car. "What the fuck is your problem? Why are you at my door?"

Shatek looked like she wanted to die. "I just wanted to buy some weed before I go to work." "No bitch. You were being smart. I ain't selling you shit! Now get the fuck off my step!"

"Really Ke? That's how you're gonna talk to me. After all we have going on, you're gonna act like that with me?" She turned and walked away with her head down low and her eyes full of tears. Ke headed back to the car and grabbed a few bags from the car. He put the stuff in the bedroom and hit the shower.

Ke yelled from the bathroom, "'Nasia, Come here please."

"Yes."

"Don't let that bitch fuck up our day. She's just mad 'cause I told her if it ain't about business then don't hit my phone."

"Okay, so you done fucking around on me now?"

"Yo, what'd I just say? Don't start! We're about to have a good day. Can we just live in the moment, please? Is the baby stuff packed and ready? She got a cup and a snack for the ride?"

"Yes, she's been ready. She's in the room watching *Blue's Clues* until her dad gets her."

"Well soon as I get dressed I am ready to go. I love it when you wear your hair like that. It makes you look even more beautiful." He finished showering and got ready to head out. He grabbed the car seat and loaded up the car. ZahNyah was ready to go. Her feet was swinging from her car seat, and she was all smiles. "Mom, I am going with my dad."

"Me too, Princess."

"Yay!"

We hit the highway and headed to Philly. Once we got to the outlets, we got the stroller and hit the stores. Baby girl picked out anything and everything she could and put it in the cart. She was such a daddy's girl. She spent most of her day in daddy's arms while the bags rode in the stroller. After hours of shopping, it was time to eat. They hit the closest restaurant, Red Lobster. They enjoyed a nice meal and headed to the car. After getting everything in the car, Ke had forgotten his phone on the table, so he ran back in to grab it. The phone was ringing as he got to the car. 'Nasia checked the ID and it said, 'Boo Thang.' Staring at the side of his face, she asked, "So you're not going to answer that?" Ke knew it would be a long ride if he fed into her shit, so he blasted the music. Baby girl was in the back seat knocked out sleep with the new bear that daddy got for her. Ky'Nasia was a little pissed but was determined to enjoy her day. She sat back and listened to the words of *Song Cry* by Jay-Z. It hit so hard that she had to play it again. Ke looked over at her, and he could see the pain in her eyes. For some reason the streets had a hold on him that just wouldn't quit.

At the house, Ke unloaded the car while 'Nasia put Sweet Pea to bed. He came in the room and gave her the bear and kissed her good night. Nasia headed to the bathroom, but Ke stopped her, "Be ready in an hour. Put that red and black shit on with the all black J's. I will be right back." Ky'Nasia looked at the clock. It was 8:35 pm. He kissed her passionately before he ran out the door with a quick, "I love you, girl." She rolled her eyes as she went to the bathroom. Her hour was almost up so 'Nasia finished putting away all the new clothes, shoes, hats, and toys they had just purchased. She ran up the stairs and hit the shower. She was dressed and ready to go without any time to spare, in fact, she was late. Another knock at the door had her gears going. She opened the door slowly to see the young girl from down the street at the door. "Is Mr. Ke here? My brother is missing, and my mom sent me down here to see if Mr. Ke knew where he was."

"He's not here. He should be back soon. I will let him know what's going on and tell him to reach out to your mom."

"You're Mr. Ke's sister?"

"No. I am his girl. Why did you say sister?"

"Oh. He's been with some other girl at my house. She's really skinny, always got weave in her hair, brown skin, no butt or titties. I think she's outside now." Ky'Nasia made sure ZahNyah was sleeping and took a walk to the corner with the young girl. "There she is right there. The one with the striped shirt and glasses." It was Shatek. Ky'Nasia nodded her head as they headed back to the house. Ke pulls up yelling, "What are you doing out here with this little ass girl? Are you ready to go?"

"Bitch, you better shut the fuck up! Who do you think you're talking to? I am grown." Her phone buzzed in her pocket. Malachi had been trying to get at her all day. They walk into the house and 'Nasia quickly checked her phone. Malachi texted, *"Damn, if I knew it would be this hard to get in touch with you, I would have kidnapped you at the gas station that day. I just want to hear from you."* A smile spread across her face. Ke stepped into the kitchen, he was ready to go. He grabbed the keys and handed 'Nasia her pocketbook. They got in the car and his bitch started her shit. She was calling his phone back to back. She sent him nude photos asking if he missed it and telling him to come get it. She was wildin'. Ke deleted all the texts and pictures.

Ky'Nasia asked, "Where are we going?"

"Sit back and relax. Daddy got you. You want to spend time with your man, right?"

"Yes."

"Alright then." Ke turned up the music and grabbed her hand. They held hands the entire ride. 'Nasia texted Malachi back, *"I will hit you up in the AM. Give me a minute."* Ke was in his own world until he saw her texting on the phone.

"That nigga better get his own Queen 'cause I ain't sharing

mines. You better tell that nigga that I play the game for real!"

"Ke relax! It ain't even that serious. He's just a friend."

"Well just a friend is gonna get his ass kicked and yours if he don't have some respect for me and my woman. It's 10:30 pm and he's hitting your line. He wants to fuck, and I ain't no dummy."

"Whatever. Thought we were enjoying the moment? You have a whole bitch sending you nudes asking if you miss it. News fucking flash! You have to have had something in order to miss it!"

"We're not about to do this."

"You're right. We're not!"

The rest of the ride to Atlantic City was quiet. The music was on full blast and the windows were down. She could smell the saltwater in the air. They hit the city and checked into their room. Ky'Nasia did her normal routine of spraying everything down with Lysol, even the bed; each layer of sheet. Ke pulled out the bottle of Henny and some weed. 'Nasia had never smoked before. Ke grabbed her ass and pulled her to him. "Let me tell you something. It's us against the world Babe. I will never let you go. You're mine and I mean that from the bottom of my heart. So, if you think this nigga is about to come in and take what belongs to me, you're buggin'."

"I am not your property, Ke. I am supposed to be your woman! The one and only woman. Now let us make the best of tonight."

"Are we going to the club or casino?"

"I don't care."

After a few shots of Henny and smoking a blunt, Ke was ready to go. Nasia took a few shots of Henny too, and they hit the door. Ke kept grabbing 'Nasia ass and saying, "That's all mine." "Nasia could tell he was drunk. While in the casino, Ke tried to suck on her titty. Ky'Nasia was getting pissed. "Let me lick your nipples baby."

"If that's what you want, let's go back to the room."

With his hands down her pants, he fingered her in the casino. Trying to fight him off, she pulled away, but not enough to get free of his grip. Ke started kissing her neck and sucking on her ear lobe. "I just want you to enjoy the moment. I want to take you places and do things to your body that you've never imagined." He pressed his fingers up against her clit, and she lost control.

She had an orgasm right there in the casino. Ke pulled his hands out of her pants and licked the nectar off his fingers. He slid one or two fingers in her mouth, so she could enjoy her juices as well. They headed back to the hotel room with Ke's hand up her shirt. Once inside the elevator, Ke exposed her breasts and began sucking on her nipples. He didn't care that there was a camera in the corner, and at this point she was too horny to care. The elevator reached their floor and opened for people to see a show. The people watched in complete shock. Ke continued to suck and finger 'Nasia's pussy. Ready to finish what he started, Ke pulled her into the room.

In the room, Ke rolled up a blunt and got in bed while 'Nasia hopped in the shower and hit the sheets. Ke handed her the Dutch and said, "Hit this." After a pull or two, 'Nasia started coughing and choking. Ke laughed, "Give me my shit. You don't know what you're doing. You're about to kill yourself." Then, like clockwork, his phone rang. Pushing it under the pillow he rolled over to put his arms around 'Nasia. "Are you good, or do you want some more?"

Feeling the head change, she told him she was good as she got comfortable in bed. With Ke's arms around her waist she felt safe. She was in her own world. Ke was dozing off and couldn't keep his eyes open. The night came to an end way too fast. The sun was up, and both of their phones were ringing. It was time to head back home, but not before they tossed around in the sheets for over an hour. 'Nasia's hair was all over the place. She quickly flat ironed her hair and wrapped it up for the ride home. In the car, Ky'Nasia's phone was going crazy. It was her mom letting her know that Malachi had been by the house looking for her. 'Nasia laughed to herself thinking 'this boy is crazy.'

Ke dropped 'Nasia off home claiming he had to make a move really quick and would be back in two hours. 'Nasia agreed to stay home while Ke handled his business. The less she knew, the better, and for her sake. 'Nasia grabbed her phone and sat on the couch to text Malachi back. *"Good morning, Sir. How are you? I was out last night. I got the message that you were looking for me at my mom's crib."*

Malachi hit back within seconds, *"I am good now that I heard from you. Can we have lunch any day this week or even a cup of tea since you don't do coffee?"*

"We can have lunch, but I am not sure when. I have a baby girl. You do know that right?"

"Yes, I know. She can come. It's not like I am trying to get in bed with you. I just want to catch up with you. Are you free now?"

"I don't have my car right now."

"I will get you a cab. Where do you want to go?"

"We can go close and quick for now, so Pizza Hut will do."

"Okay. A cab is on the way. See you when you get there."

'Nasia rushed to get her and ZahNyah ready to go. The cab pulled up and 'Nasia's phone rang. It was Ke letting her know that he wouldn't be done in two hours. He said it would be more like four to five hours. That made her wonder why it would take that long, but she just agreed and hung up.

At Pizza Hut, Malachi opened the cab door and led them to their seats. He held the door open and pulled out their chairs. He was the opposite of RahKe. He allowed the ladies to order first and made sure they got whatever they wanted. ZahNyah was mad because she couldn't drink everyone's drink. She enjoyed her meal and made a mess at the same time. When was time to go, no one wanted to leave. The conversation was so real. They agreed to do it again real soon as Malachi closed the door to the cab and they drove off.

She was back home in three hours, and Ke still wasn't there. The sun was beginning to set, and it was almost dark out. 'Nasia was getting worried so she called Ke. "Hey, are you good?"

"Yeah, I will be there in a minute. Just relax. I got something for you when I get there."

"Okay, I wanted to make sure you were safe. I'll see you when you get here." Laying down on the sofa, she listened as the rain softly beat on the roof. Wrapped up in her blanket, she drifted off to sleep. She felt him tugging on the covers as he kissed her neck. 'Nasia opened her eyes slightly as he lifted up her T-shirt. His hands slid up to her breasts. As he began to play with her nipples, he continued kissing on her neck. She moaned softly as her temperature started to rise. Gently caressing her thighs, he took off his clothes. The rain began to pour down harder setting the mood for a good pounding. Fingering her sweet heaven, they kissed roughly and passionately. His tongue danced around her nipples and then it traveled down to her sweet spot. As he sucked on her pussy, her body was grinding to his beat. Her hands massaged the back of his head as he pushed as much of her pussy that would fit into his mouth. She pulled him up to her so her tongue do the talking. It bounced around his neck like wildfire tracing down to his manhood. Starting at the tip of Big Daddy, she slowly licked it up and down. It was hard as a rock. She sucked it for a little while longer as his toes began to curl, and his hands gripped the sofa as if to hold onto his nut a little longer. She licked all the precum and left Big Daddy clean. Mounting Kong for the ride of her life, she was ready. Riding that dick like a Stallion, they were both in ecstasy. He flipped her over, so he could hit it doggie-style. Entering her from behind, he grabbed her hips and jammed his entire dick inside her. Feeling it damn near in her throat, she yelled out in pain and in pleasure. His thrusts got harder, rougher, and faster as he fucked her like his life depended on it. Screams of pure pleasure left her mouth with every stroke. Her nectar ran down her legs. "It feels so good. It's deep baby. Slow down," she cried.

"Tell me you love this dick."

"I love this dick, Daddy." As the words left her mouth, his dick jammed into her farther and harder. Every stroke got deeper and harder. Her body was losing control. Their senses heightened as they got deeper into each other. She squeezed the back of his legs tighter as he continued to pound away. He turned her onto her back and threw her legs over his shoulders. He took his time in her caramel center. He wanted to make love for a few moments, and he gave her sweet pleasure. The rain had lightened up and changed the mood and they just grooved with it. Fiending for more, she began to throw her body up against his. Seeing the hunger in her eyes, he pulled her hips in and took complete control. Screaming for more, he fucked her with every bit of strength he had. He gave it to her rough and without mercy. Her legs were spread apart, and he bounced in and out with force. She busted so many nuts back to back it was like an ocean of juices flowing from between her legs. Wrapping her legs around his waist, they were in sync grinding together. Feeling Kong swell up inside her, she knew he was ready. With harder and harder thrusts, they both climaxed together, and nut was running all down her ass. The pool of nut under her ass was huge. Slowing down to a stop, he could barely breathe when he whispered in her ear, "I love you, baby." Laying beside her, they listened to the rain as the storm became quieter.

'Nasia's phone rang. When she woke up, no one was there. It was only a dream. She grabbed her phone to see who was calling, but the caller ID said, 'unknown.' She answered as she checked the time, "Hello?" It was 2:45 am when she was hit with a familiar blow to the heart.

"This is Shatek. RahKe is here with me. He is asleep. He passed out after I put him down. A bad bitch always knows how to put her man to bed. Anyway, Ke and I have been fucking for three months now but seeing each other for four months. He gives me rides to work in your car. He also makes sure I have good smoke and lunch to take to work from time to time. I can't just leave him alone. I love him just like you do. I just thought you should know because I am tired of being a secret. He said he loves me."

“Where are you at? Put Ke on the phone!” The dial tone rung in her ear. The bitch hung up.

Round 8

Sparing Through Fatigue

As 'Nasia fought in round eight with two contenders, she was hit with a mind-blowing sucker punch to her right eye. While checking RahKe's voicemail, she heard Shatek saying that she missed his presence and needed to feel him. Feel him though! That meant there was physical contact yet again. Talk about a slap in the face.

'Nasia was left in the crib every night, so he could go chill with other women. It hurt, and the pain from the first round returned as if it never left. 'Nasia had to figure out what was happening to her and that piece of their relationship. The cycle of coming and going was becoming too much for her.

After not being able to hold down her favorite meal down of fried fish, baked mac and cheese, and candied yams for three weeks in a row, she took a trip to the hospital. The nurse walked in with a cup in her hand, asking for a urine sample and then took a few blood samples. It seemed like it took hours for the results to come back. The nurse came in to tell Ky'Nasia what was wrong, but she seemed very happy and cheerful to share some news that would change Ky'Nasia's world. 'Nasia was confused because all she wanted to do was eat, but she couldn't. The doctor walked in smiling and also happy.

"We have good news, and we have bad news. Which would you like to hear first?"

"The bad news please." All kinds of crazy things were going through her head. All the "what ifs" came rushing in at once. She laid there still as the world around her paused and she said a quick prayer. "Lord, please don't let me have any STDs. Especially the ones that don't have a cure. Amen." She took a breath.

As the doctor began to talk, he snapped her out of it by saying, "The bad news is that you are very dehydrated, and we have to give you IV fluids. Which means you have to sit here for at least another hour to get fluids. The good news is that you're two months pregnant. We will be doing an ultrasound to make sure the baby is okay because of all of the bleeding you are having. Other than that, you are healthy and well."

A feeling of relief and shock consumed her as her jaw hit the floor and her head started spinning. "Now, I am about to have two kids and no father in their life. This ain't right. Do another test after you give me the fluids." The doctor agreed to do a blood test on her so she could be sure.

The drive to the house was a blur as she continued to replay the doctor's words in her head. What was she going to do? Ke was facing thirty years to life in prison. She was working, but that wasn't enough to take care of her and two kids. She wondered if she should keep it and it weighed heavy on her heart, but she knew that abortion wasn't an option.

Entering the house, she went straight to the shower and

right to bed. RahKe came home and asked her what happened at the hospital. She told him she was dehydrated and needed fluids and rest.

"I think you should get rest and take off work for a few days. Also, you're leaving something out. What else did they say?"

"Nothing. Why do you think that?"

"So, you're not pregnant?" Ke lifts her head so he could look her into the eyes.

As the tears began to fall, 'Nasia said, "Not sure what I'm going to do about that."

"If you think you getting rid of my baby you're stupid. You ain't killing nothing I made."

"Nigga did you forget you're facing LIFE in prison? Who is going to help me raise two kids? Please don't say your family! They all fucked up and are struggling just like me."

"You heard what the fuck I said. What do you want for dinner that you can eat? I am about to get us dinner then, I will be here to rest with you."

Rolling her eyes Ky'Nasia pulled the covers over her head and turned over. Ke walked out of the room and the door slammed behind him. RahKe thinking he could control her body was driving her crazy and stressing her out. She laid in bed and cried herself to sleep.

Ke came bursting into the room with crackers, Ginger Ale, and a sub from the Wawa. As he pulled the blankets off 'Nasia, she checked the time. It was 10:30 pm. 'This nigga is nuts,' she thought to herself as she pulled the blankets back up over her head. Ke sat at the foot of the bed trying to get his shit together. "You're gonna eat something. You're not about to starve my baby or yourself. I got you some crackers and Ginger Ale in case your stomach still fucked up."

"Ke don't nobody want to eat at twelve o'clock midnight. You left here at 4 pm talking about getting dinner. What? You had to grow the animals to get the meat and cheese for Wawa? I must be the dumbest motherfucker alive. I ate already! Leave the crackers and Ginger Ale on the nightstand. You can go back to your whore. She let me know you were there."

"'Nasia stop your bullshit. We're not about to go through this every day. You've got to take care of yourself so the baby can be good. The doctor said stress ain't good for the baby."

"Then why are you stressing me the fuck out? Why am I getting phone calls from your bitches letting me know you will be home soon 'cause you just left their house?"

"Don't worry about that! I am taking care of her. You know the bitch will say anything to piss you off and keep you mad at me. I just need to make sure you're good. I love you and my kids. I need y'all to be straight."

"Whatever RahKe! I am so sick of dealing with this bullshit. I just want out. I don't want to be your girl anymore. I need the space you refuse to take. I am done!"

"Okay, 'Nasia. If that's what you want, then fuck it. But I ain't leaving you here with my babies to struggle and stress. I will be here every step of the way."

Days went by and Ke was in and out. He stayed out a few

nights in a row and would call to check up on 'Nasia and the kids. 'Nasia continued to work and bust her ass to provide for her and her kids. She was determined to make it without Ke's help.

At work, 'Nasia started to feel weak. She had been bleeding for five days straight, so she decided to go to the hospital. Only ten weeks pregnant, she was very concerned about the amount of blood she was losing. Ky'Nasia explained to the doctor what she had been experiencing. The doctor ordered all types of bloodwork and tests. Without any warning, she felt an unexpected, yet painful blow that left her speechless. The ultrasound showed no heartbeat and no baby. Tears streamed down her face like a river as the doctor confirmed her miscarriage. Stuck in shock mode, 'Nasia sat still as the doctor finished his exam and treated her to prevent infections. Ky'Nasia left the hospital at 2:43 am. She got home to see Ke sitting on the step with some chick.

"So, you're out fucking while you're carrying my seed! You've got to be stupid."

"Fuck you Ke and your bitch too." She slammed the paperwork from the hospital into his chest. RahKe read the paperwork and instantly came into the house. Rushing into the bathroom to hold 'Nasia, he watched as she stripped off her clothing one piece at a time as the tears continued to fall. Ke grabbed her gently from behind and whispered "I am so sorry, baby. I love you."

'Nasia held on to the wall as she tried to get a grip on life. "Please leave me alone. I don't want to be bothered and your chick is waiting for you. I just need to shower and go to bed. In fact, do you have any weed? I think I need a blunt to help me sleep."

"Yeah. I got something for you. Let me get a Dutch out of the car. I am going to stay here with you tonight. You work tomorrow?"

"Doctor took me out of work for a week. I don't know what happened."

"It's all my fault. I have to stop this shit. It's hurting my family. I am really sorry. I will have the Dutch rolled when you get out the shower. Where is ZahNyah?"

"She's at your mom's house 'cause I worked a double today."

The look on his face changed to anger. "Didn't the doctor tell you before to slow down on working all of those shifts! You're so fucking stubborn and hardheaded. Did you prove your point now?" He stormed out of the bathroom. 'Nasia got in the shower with the thought of it being her fault too. Did she cause this too? She let the hot water beat down on her back as tears fell from her face. They hit the water like a brick. Her heart sank to her feet the more she thought about what Ke had said. Stepping out of the shower she felt really weak. She made it to the bed and Ke was in the kitchen cooking french fries and fried chicken wings.

"Do you want some of this food? You want me to make you a plate?"

"No. Where is the lighter? I just want to go to sleep. I am tired and my body hurts."

"It's on the nightstand next to the candles." Ke came rushing into the room to avoid being locked out. He placed his food on the dresser and went to grab something to drink. He fixed the bed the way he liked and then got in. Trying to feel her out, he watched as Ky'Nasia smoked the blunt. Knowing he wanted some, she passed it to him after she was finished. "You must really be hurt 'cause you've never smoked this much. I am here if you want to talk or be held. I know you like to be cuddled up when you're going through something."

"I mean, I just lost my baby. I wasn't sure if I wanted to keep it at first, but once I got over the initial shock I was okay with having another baby. I guess the stress and working like a dog got the best of me. I never intended to kill my baby." The tears streamed down as RahKe held her close.

"I am so sorry. I wish I could do something to change it and the way you feel. I have to be a better person for you and my kids. This shit hurts man." RahKe rubbed her back while handing her the blunt. Ky'Nasia took a few more pulls and was done. She wrapped herself up in the covers as Ke finished off the blunt and his plate of food. Still in shock, 'Nasia grabbed the pillow and held it tight. RahKe reached over and rubbed her stomach and legs. He scooted in close to her and held her. He kissed the back of her neck softly and they drifted off to sleep in each other's arms.

The next morning, RahKe got up and made breakfast for Ky'Nasia. He had even gotten her fresh orange juice. He set her breakfast on the nightstand too. That morning, he waited on her hand and foot. 'Nasia ate breakfast in bed and watched TV. RahKe joined her after cleaning the kitchen and rolling his blunt. They shared their feelings with one another and talked about how to move forward from there. RahKe explained that he had a few things to do that morning and that he would be back soon.

Ky'Nasia took a nap after Ke left. She woke up around 1:30 pm to the house still being empty. She cleaned her room while listening to slow jams. Before she knew it, it was 5:45 pm and Ke wasn't back and hadn't even called. She jumped in the shower, then prepared dinner. While dinner was cooking, she called for ZahNyah to come home. RahKe's mom said she would bring her home tomorrow so 'Nasia could get one more day of good rest. ZahNyah told Ky'Nasia how much fun she was having and that she missed her mom. They said their 'I love you's' and hung up the phone. 'Nasia was exhausted so she ate dinner and curled up in bed watching TV until she dozed off again.

RahKe returned home at 11:20 pm that night. He was so drunk and high that he left his phone on the step. Ke came in the room trying to explain why he was late getting back to Ky'Nasia, but she wasn't interested in hearing his lies. "RahKe please stop the bullshit! I really don't care, nor do I want to hear any more of your lies. This is part of the reason we're in this situation. I just want to heal and try to move on. You can sleep in the living room tonight."

"Ky'Nasia, I am sorry. This shit hurt me, too. I had a few drinks with the fellows after I told them what had happened to you and the baby. I just wanted to clear my head. I need to be okay so I can help you."

"You're funny! Help me how?" Ky'Nasia showed RahKe the picture of him and Shatek cuddled up on her couch. "I don't need your help. This is how you help me? Damn, I just lost the baby yesterday and today you're laid up with your side piece. It's amazing how things work out. Hope she's as good as this picture show 'cause she has some big shoes to fill. I would appreciate it if you left and only came around when you're needed for our daughter." Ky'Nasia slammed his phone into his chest and went to the bathroom. She cried for a good while then got herself together and went to bed.

RahKe laid across the foot of the bed trying to make her understand that he doesn't know how to be a good man. He told her that he never had a good example of what a good man was or what one did." He began to rub her feet and kiss them. "I worship the ground you walk on and the Earth you live in. Please give me another chance to prove it to you. I want you. I want this." RahKe grabbed Ky'Nasia and held her close. He could hear and feel her crying.

"What you are saying sounds really good and all, but it's the same things you've been saying. Ain't nothing changed. I am mentally tired of the rerun. I can't do this shit no more."

"I will show you this time. Actions speak louder than words, right? Let me do the work. Please trust me this time." RahKe grabbed his phone and deleted Shatek's number and all her messages.

'Nasia rolled her eyes. "Why are we wasting our time? You know that number by heart. The same way I know yours. Please stop with the games." She grabbed her phone as it continued to buzz on the dresser and looked at the message. Looking like she had seen a ghost, she handed Ke the phone. It was photos of him and Shatek nude, sent from Shatek herself. Her stomach instantly felt sick. She deleted the photos and moved to the top of the bed.

RahKe began to explain, "They are old pictures. I don't know why I took them. I ain't even into that girl like that. She was just a jump-off, but she gives me so much attention. She always wants me. I guess I got caught up in the groupie phase."

Ky'Nasia was over it. She laid in bed staring at the ceiling. Thoughts of giving up on everything consumed her mind. Resting in her home was all she cared about at that moment as her eyes drifted shut. RahKe heard her snoring and covered her up. Laying beside her was good enough for him at that time. Knowing that she was really hurt by the pictures, Ke decided to do something special for her.

The days seemed to fly by as Ky'Nasia returned to work the following week. She went back with a vengeance. She worked doubles four days a week. She never was home. All work and no play was her motto, as she took care of ZahNyah and herself. She came home from work one day to find RahKe and his boys on her porch. She walked by and spoke to everyone as she entered the house. Ke followed her in asking why she was late getting home from work.

"What makes you think I have to answer that? You must have bumped your head somewhere," Ky'Nasia said with a confused look on her face. She continued to put away the food she had just purchased from Shoprite.

"Are there more bags in the car?"

"Yes. I will go get them when I am done with these."

"I will get them. I need to use the car for a bit."

"I bet you do. It's always something you need when you come around."

RahKe took the car and left while Ky'Nasia cooked dinner. Trying not to watch the clock, she got ZahNyah ready for bed after they ate dinner. They laid in the living room watching TV until ZahNyah fell asleep. 'Nasia got in the shower with the door open so she could hear if ZahNyah woke up. Listening to her slow jams, she never heard Ke enter the bathroom. As she was soaping up her washcloth, RahKe entered the shower from the back. He grabbed her softly from behind and whispered in her ear, "Damn, I miss seeing this body naked. I just want to hold you a few minutes." He ran his hands across her back.

Ky'Nasia was shocked he had come back at a decent hour. Trying not to get excited about a moment that would probably begin with sex and end with him exiting to be with another woman, she started washing her body from head to toe. Ke got his rag and washed her back and then his body. Not wanting to look at Ke, Ky'Nasia stayed with her back towards him. She could feel him breathing on her neck. Ke reached over and kissed her neck. He planted kisses down her spine and back up. Reaching around, he massaged her titties, one in each hand. Still a sucker for RahKe, she felt weak in his hands. She didn't want to give in, but she couldn't help herself. Before she knew it, her fingers were in her sweet spot. Ke knew his magic would affect her that way so he was ready for whatever. Sliding his hands into her heaven, he slowly pushed his fingers inside after moving her hands out of the way. He played with her heaven until she could barely stand. He scooped her up and wrapped her legs around him as the water beat down on both of them. Ky'Nasia wrapped her arms around his neck as she enjoyed his presence. Ke slid his dick inside her caramel square. 'Nasia let out a sigh of pleasure. She hadn't felt Ke inside her for four long weeks. It felt so damn good. Her pussy instantly gushed with juices. "Damn, I miss this shit," Ke whispered in her ear. Gripping her ass tighter as he pushed Kong deeper into her. "This shit feels like heaven. Promise me this my pussy and you will never give it away."

"This shit feels too good. Please slow down. I need you to go easy on me. It's your pussy baby, but I don't want to share anymore."

"You don't have to. Do you feel how hard this dick is? That's all for you, baby. I promise."

"Just fuck me. Don't make promises you can't keep."

They continued to fuck as Ke placed his finger on her lips

to shush her. Ky'Nasia asked Ke, "Fuck me from the back, but do it slowly." RahKe turned her around slowly as he lifted her leg up on the edge of the tub. 'Nasia leaned forward as Ke slowly entered her from behind. She jumped a little as Kong hit her spot. Feeling the rush of juices sliding down his dick, Ke gripped her breast and pinched her nipples. 'Nasia's body quivered at the touch of RahKe. He smiled as he felt her nut release from her body. She had no control over the way her body responded to him. Ke sucked and licked all over her neck.

"Baby, can I please fuck? I want to feel you. I need this pussy. I miss it and you." He stroked nice and slow as she could hear the pleading in his voice. She forced her sweet spot onto him roughly. Ke gripped her ass. Bending over she grabbed her ankles as Ke prepared to fuck her rough. Not sure if she was ready she took a deep breath and held it for a few seconds. She released it with a yell of pleasure and pain as Ke fucked her rough and fast from the back. She let go of her ankles and held on to the wall. She braced herself for the force she knew Ke would use. He wanted to make sure that pussy was his. RahKe fucked 'Nasia like it was his last time on Earth. The thrusts became harder and faster as Ke began to swell up inside her. Not wanting the ride to be over, she asked if she could ride him cowgirl style.

Ready to watch that ass bounce on that dick, he quickly said, "Yes." Ke sat in the tub while 'Nasia got herself together and squatted down on Kong. The feeling of pure pleasure shot to her brain and a loud moan left her lips. She rode that dick like it was a bull. Ke's dicked swelled up big and thick as his nut mounted up inside of him. She heard Ke lose control, and he busted a nut. It shot inside Ky'Nasia like hot lava. They sat in the tub as they got their breathing under control. They held hands and talked for a few seconds until their bodies realized the water was as cold as ice.

'Nasia took a quick shower and got out of the tub. RahKe followed suite and got ready for bed. Ky'Nasia was getting dressed when RahKe stepped out of the room to take a phone call. Rolling her eyes, he came into the room grabbing his clothes to leave. "I have to make a run real fast. I will be back in less than an hour."

Ky'Nasia checked on ZahNyah and placed her in bed. After cleaning up the kitchen, 'Nasia laid in bed watching *Tom and Jerry* until she dozed off. RahKe returned home three hours later and slid in bed. Ky'Nasia could smell the weed and alcohol on his breath. She tucked the covers under her because she just wanted to sleep. RahKe passed out within minutes. They slept facing the opposite side each other listening to RahKe's phone ringing all night.

Round 9

Tag Team Trouble

Blow after blow, Ky'Nasia endured round nine against an opponent who danced in the ring like Mike Tyson as he gave her forceful body blows to her ribs. Even at work, she would get word saying, 'your nigga fuck with some girl from The House of Panties! I see your car there all the time.' Shocked, she asked for the address. She pulled up to the address late at night after work and found out that it was Shatek's house. Pissed to know that RahKe was still dealing with that bitch, 'Nasia pulled off and went home. Fresh out of the shower, Ky'Nasia was prepared to snuggle up in bed with ZahNyah. She called RahKe to see where he was at, but he didn't pick up the phone. She called Ke's mother to find out where ZahNyah was and she was with her. She told her to pick ZahNyah up tomorrow morning.

The next morning, she still hadn't heard from RahKe. Ky'Nasia got dressed and went to The House of Panties. 'Nasia hit the corner and RahKe was sitting on the step with Shatek in between his legs. He saw Ky'Nasia turn the corner and ran like he had seen a ghost. 'Nasia pulled up on him and he began to explain. "Baby it's not what it looks like. We were just smoking. I ain't fuck her today."

"That was next I guess. Why aren't you answering your phone? I am too tired to even deal with this shit."

Ky'Nasia went to Ke's mom's house and got the baby. On the way home, Ky'Nasia started feeling sharp pains in her back and stomach. She pulled over trying to wait for the pain to pass. She had been ducking an dodging punches and guessed that the last strike had hit her a little too hard. She thought she was all worked up about Ke still fucking with Shatek, but this pain was different. Once she felt a little better, she went home. She balled up into a knot to try and ease the pain as she slept. The next morning the pain was unbearable. She called RahKe phone and asked him to get the baby so she could go to the hospital, but he ended up being the one to take her there.

Sitting in the ER with pain shooting from her stomach to her back, tears fell down her face. When she saw the doctor, he announced that she was five months pregnant. She passed out from the news. They hooked her up and put her on all types of IV fluids and ran a million tests. She was completely stunned. RahKe was there holding her hand every step of the way. Ky'Nasia was flipping out. "I was just told two and a half months ago that I had a miscarriage and I was treated for it. Now you're telling me that my baby NEVER died and that I am five months pregnant. I've been living life like I don't have a baby growing inside me! I've been dancing, drinking, and smoking, not to mention working four to five doubles a week." She started to feel lightheaded again, so the doctor and Ke told her to relax.

"We are going to run more tests and keep you overnight to make sure the baby is healthy and safe. You will receive IV fluids overnight because you are very dehydrated, and your blood volume is low."

Ke was concerned too. “She was receiving a high dose of antibiotics. How will that affect the baby? Will it affect the baby? Should we be worried?”

“We are about to check all that out now. I was reviewing her records while the nurse was setting up her IV. The tech will be here to take her to get an ultrasound so we can check the growth and if there are any issues with the baby. There shouldn’t be any issues, but just to be on the safe side, we want to monitor her more closely.” The doctor exited the room and put his plan into motion. He had people coming in and out of the room doing all kinds of workups.

Knowing that she was trapped in the hospital for the night made her really scared. RahKe promised to be there the entire time. He went to the store to get them a bite to eat, but Ky’Nasia couldn’t eat until the results of some of the tests came back. After an hour of tests, they cleared her to eat, but she still wasn’t free to go home. Ky’Nasia nerves were bad. She had bit off all her nails and was shaking like a leaf. RahKe reached over and rubbed her back telling her she would be fine and that everything was going to be good. He got on the bed to hold her. She was too scared to stop him.

The tech took her to the ultrasound room and the baby was in there swimming from side to side. Everything appeared to be normal. They both breathed a sigh of relief as they watched their baby in amusement. Ke kissed her forehead and then her belly. The ultrasound went great. At least that's what they thought. Back in the room, RahKe was on the phone texting letting everyone know the baby was good. The doctor peeked in the room, “I will be back to discuss your results in a few minutes. I am waiting on two more tests to clear.”

It was 5:42 am and the doctor wasn’t back yet. A nurse

walked in and set up some medicine for her IV and drew more blood. She rubbed her hand across 'Nasia's belly and said, "It's going to be alright. It will be well." Then she walked out.

The doctor came rushing in at a quarter after six in the morning. "Good morning. I have some bad news and good news. The baby is okay, but it has bacteria growing in its intestines that needs to be treated now with a one-time dose of antibiotics and again once it is born. However, the baby is developing fine. There are no issues or concerns with the development of the baby at this time. The nurse started you on the medicine that was needed. It will run for an hour and then you can leave. Instead of following up with your doctor once a month, I want you to go every two weeks starting next week. You are to come here every Friday to get the baby's intestines checked now until delivery. Do you understand or do you have any questions?"

RahKe was nervous, but he had her back. "I will be sure she gets wherever she needs to be Doc. Should she be working? She works a lot of hours and with heavy chemicals. There's a lot of heavy lifting also."

"She shouldn't work right now. She needs to be on bed rest for the next two weeks and then she can go on light duty until she goes out to have the baby. That will give the baby time to develop and adjust to the antibiotics. There's nothing to worry about right now. Just make sure you follow the restrictions I wrote out in your discharge summary. If you have any questions or need anything don't hesitate to call or come back."

RahKe squeezed Ky'Nasia hand, "We are going to be okay. I got us. The baby will be fine. I love y'all. All of y'all." He rubbed her belly and kissed it several times. They got their stuff together and left the hospital at 11:30 am. Feeling drained, they went home. Ky'Nasia hit the shower and went to bed. RahKe came in to get her order for lunch and dinner. He made cheesesteaks and fries for lunch and fried chicken, corn, and white rice for dinner. 'Nasia knew that meant he wasn't coming back any time soon. She sat in bed and ate her lunch while watching TV. RahKe showered and hit the streets.

Ky'Nasia was confused about how she didn't know she was still pregnant. She called her doctor and set up her next two appointments. She made it her business to follow what the doctor said that time around. She faxed her paperwork to her job concerning her bed rest and light duty. She was off for the next two weeks and it was time to prepare for her baby which was due on November 12th, 2006. She was praying for a boy. She took a nap after handling all of her business. She woke up at 3:30 pm and RahKe still wasn't there. She called his mother and asked her to bring baby girl over when she got home. She got up and got a snack because she didn't want to eat dinner that early.

Ky'Nasia heard a loud buzzing in the kitchen and saw RahKe's phone on the charger. She grabbed it and answered it. "Hey Daddy. What time are you picking me up? I am ready now?"

"He's not here and who is this? Where was he supposed to be picking you up from?"

Shatek laughed. "My bad. He just pulled up. I told you I can't leave him alone because I love him. He must feel the same way because he keeps coming back. Bye, I am getting in your car now. Hey Ke. What took you so long? You know Ky'Nasia answering your phone? Here she goes on the phone now."

RahKe didn't say a word. He just hung up on her. Ky'Nasia was over the bullshit. Knowing she couldn't react the way she wanted to, she took a few deep breaths and packed Ke's shit. She wasted no time bagging up all his clothes, shoes, and hats. When she was finished, she started carrying them to the hallway. RahKe came flying into the house. "Baby, please wait. It's not what you think. I was only with her to get a couple of dollars out of her so I could help pay some of these bills. Please listen to me. I don't want that girl."

"RahKe you are mad disrespectful! You're riding that bitch around in my car after you've been fucking. You spend more time with her than me and in my shit that I pay for. You're buggin." She snatched her keys out of his hand and dragged a few bags to the car. After loading all his shit in the car, Ky'Nasia droped RahKe and his belongings off at his mother's house. Ky'Nasia was finally fed up. She needed a break from RahKe and all his bullshit. She started focusing on her and her needs. 'Nasia started allowing men to take her on dates just to get her mind off RahKe, who was living his best life. Ky'Nasia started talking to Dre. He was a corny nigga, but he seemed to have his shit together. She hung out with him trying to make RahKe jealous, but the shit backfired.

She went to Dre's house one night to have dinner. After dinner, they sat on the bed watching a movie and Dre started kissing her neck. Ky'Nasia wasn't letting anyone kiss her on the mouth. Her lips were for her babies. He said he understood and continued kissing and sucking on her neck and then on her breasts. Ky'Nasia wasn't trying to have sex. She was six months pregnant for goodness sake. Dre tried to get in her pants anyway, but she wasn't having that. He sucked on her breast for a little longer and he started to lick around her waist. Her pussy was wet. It had been a while since she and RahKe had sex. She was jonesing but wasn't ready for him. He settled for being able to eat her pussy. Man, he went in head first! He even ate her ass. He slid her ass cheeks apart and sucked her ass after she nutted in his mouth a few times. 'Nasia felt uncomfortable, so she got up and went home. RahKe was there waiting and he was pissed.

"Why are you coming home at 5 am when you're pregnant with my seed? Don't make me fuck you and that nigga up. I will kill for mine."

"RahKe shut the fuck up! You don't want to be with me. You're with Shatek. Why are you even here?"

"Because our daughter wanted to come home with mommy. She said she wanted to sleep in her own bed, so I brought her home. So, did you fuck him?"

"No, did you fuck her? Don't come in here asking questions. You can't handle the truth. I am grown and I don't have to answer to you." She jumped in the shower and washed the thought of Dre eating her out of her mind.

RahKe came into the room and ripped the covers off of Ky'Nasia. "Are you even going to ask where your daughter is? Oh, you don't give a damn."

"Ke, I talked to your mom already. She told me you just dropped the baby off an hour ago and for me not to come waking her up. She will call me when she is ready for me to come to get her." Ky'Nasia rolled her eyes as she snatched the covers out of his hands.

RahKe leaned in and put his finger in her forehead. "Don't fuck with me, 'Nasia. You know how I am coming. I'll go stupid behind you." He got in the bed and rubbed her stomach. "How's my baby doing?" Ke slid his hands straight to her pussy. He kissed and sucked all over her neck and titties. She craved his touch. Her pussy was instantly soaked. She tried to push his hands away, but Ke continued to play with her clit. Juices flooded his hand. Ke went down to get himself a taste. He sucked and bit on her pussy extra rough. She pushed his head away as she begged him to stop. Ke took pleasure in her trying to get her pussy out of his mouth. Ke licked it from top to bottom. She let her juices flow like a river. He climbed on top of her and put her legs on his shoulders. He fucked her fast and hard. His breathing was heavy and out of control. He flipped her over onto her stomach and entered her from the back. His dick was huge and brick hard. He fucked her relentlessly. He busted inside her like a pop-top. He was so out of breath.

"Baby don't get nobody hurt. I love you and miss you. I want my family. Can't nobody take my family from me."

"But you! Do you think what you do is cool? That shit hurts. It fucks up my whole day. Then you have the nerve to be fucking local whores. Bottom bitches! But I guess that's what makes you a man." Cleaning herself up she laid in bed. She watched TV until they both dozed off. They had dinner as a family that night. Ke tried to make sure Ky'Nasia didn't have time to see anybody else.

Dre texted the phone and made plans for the weekend. On Friday they were going to have a seafood dinner, and Dre was going to cook it. When the week came to an end, RahKe left and went back to his normal routine. Ky'Nasia knew RahKe would only hang tight with her until the weekend. He left right after her hospital visit. 'Nasia got her outfit ready for the evening. She showered and shaved and waited for the time to pass. Two hours flew by quickly. 'Nasia rushed to get ready because she had lost track of time.

After getting dressed, she texted Dre to make sure they were still on for the night. He texted back and confirmed with a picture of the meal and its setup. She drove across town and dropped ZahNyah off to her grandma's house. She reached Dre's house and had a sudden change of heart. Not sure if she wanted to go in, she sat in the car listening to music. Dre came to the door three times before she decided to go inside. He met her at the door with arms wide open. She hugged him back and entered the house.

At the dinner table, there were candles, wine, shrimp, snow crabs, corn, potatoes, fried fish, and chicken wings. They sat down to eat, enjoyed dinner, and talked for a little longer. Feeling tired, Ky'Nasia was getting ready to go. Dre asked her to stay and watch a movie with him. Against her better judgment, she stayed to watch the movie. Dre put on *Love and Basketball*. She was cold, so he handed her a blanket and cuddled up under her. Once she got warm, it was hard for her to keep her eyes open. Dre removed her shoes from her feet and began to massage them. That was really pushing her over the top, especially since her feet were the size of balloons. She drifted in and out for a while. Finally, she passed out. Dre figured this was his chance to get her. He removed the covers and unsnapped her bra. Sucking on her titties while trying to pull down her pants, Ky'Nasia woke up. She asked, "What are you doing?"

Dre assumed she would be cool with him doing what he wanted, so he told her he just wanted to suck on her pussy for a few minutes. 'Nasia wasn't in the mood for any of that. She told him she was about to leave because she had to get her daughter. Ky'Nasia started getting herself together and Dre told her to relax. She listened because she was really tired. She dozed off again. That time she was stretched out across the bed, so it made it easier for him to slide her pants down. Ky'Nasia felt very weak. She felt like she was drugged. She could see him pulling on her pants but had no strength to stop him. Dre was sucking and licking the inner parts of her thighs. She was pissed at herself for even staying there. She didn't want to do this. "Dre stop. I am ready to go home."

"Come on, stop acting like that. Doesn't it feel good? Look how wet this shit is. I just want to feel it. I promise to be gentle."

"No. I don't want to do this. What did you do to my food or my drink? I feel funny."

"Oh, nothing. Lay back you will be fine in a little bit."

"I have to go home."

"It wouldn't be smart to drive home right now. You might not make it. Now open those legs so I can see what all the hype is about."

"What hype and what did you give me? I am pregnant and if anything hurts my baby..." Ky'Nasia blacked out. When she awoke, Dre was inside her raw. The tears rolled down her face as she tried to push him off. "Please stop. You're hurting me and I don't want to have sex with you."

"Shut the fuck up and take this dick. Did you really think I was going to eat your pussy without getting some ass? Oh, you really thought somebody would buy all that seafood and not get any ass? Take this dick and shut up."

Feeling really disrespected and low, Ky'Nasia laid there and cried. It was times like that she had wished she would have listened to RahKe. She wanted so badly to call him to come to her rescue, but she knew what he would say and do. She cried until it was over. After he nutted, Dre grabbed a towel and threw it at 'Nasia. "I busted in you 'cause you're already pregnant so I don't have to worry about you saying that shit is mine. Clean yourself up and you can let yourself out. I am going to sleep. I have to go to work in a few hours."

Ky'Nasia cleaned herself up as best she could. She was still a little weak and out of it. After dressing herself, she headed down the steps and sat on the couch. She tried to regroup so Ke wouldn't notice that something was wrong. She drove home in silence. She got home and ran straight to the shower. She used all the hot water and allowed it to burn her skin. Feeling less than a woman, she wished she was never born. She sat in the tub until the water turned cold. She washed her entire body in bleach. Her skin was burning, but she didn't care. She felt disgusted. Exiting the shower, she put on two layers of clothes to try and hide how she felt inside. She laid in bed as the tears continued to fall.

She heard someone at the door, so she wiped her face and got herself together. RahKe busted in the room. "You're gonna keep fucking with me until I kill your dumb ass. Ain't you? Where the fuck were you all night?"

"I went somewhere I shouldn't have gone." The tears welled up in her eyes. "I am sorry. I will listen from now on. I promise." The tears began to flow as 'Nasia told RahKe what happened, but he laughed.

"You're a whore just like the rest of them. You're out having dates and fucking while you pregnant with my seed. What the fuck is wrong with you?"

"Ke he raped me! I said no. I think he put something in my food or drink because I was weak and felt funny. I started to call you to come and get me, but I didn't want you to get in trouble. He took it. I swear I didn't want to have sex with him. He forced me, but I guess it's my fault because I went over there. It's my fault for wanting someone to love me and want to spend time with me. I was desperate for attention and this is what I get. Raped." Seeing the disgust in RahKe's eyes made her cry even harder.

"Fuck you whore. You took another nigga's dick raw while you were pregnant with my child. The same child you almost lost. You're a grimy bitch. I hope he's ready to play daddy because that ain't my fucking baby no more. Fuck you for real." RahKe stormed back out of the house. Ky'Nasia cried so long and so hard she caused herself to have an asthma attack. RahKe had never talked to her in that manner. She felt sick. She laid there trying to get it together, but she couldn't. She cried herself to sleep.

Ky'Nasia woke up at 1:50 pm. She had sharp pain running up her side. She went to the hospital and they ran more tests. The doctor came in with a weird look on his face. "You have an STD and a UTI. They are both curable with antibiotics. You are also dehydrated. It is summertime, so you must drink more fluids. We will give you your first dose of antibiotics here and a script for the rest. Take one tablet three times a day for seven days. No sex for fourteen days and tell your partner so they can be treated as well. We are going to run a bag of fluids in you via IV. I want an ultrasound to check on the baby then you will be free to go."

After everything that happened, Ky'Nasia called RahKe and told him to go get checked. He snapped and called her more names. When 'Nasia got home, Ke was on the porch. He had fire in his eyes. "Bitch you're trying to kill my seed. Now you got a fucking STD and trying to blame me. Bitch my dick is clean. Fuck you whore." He grabbed her car keys and left. Ky'Nasia went and laid on the couch. She watched the fish swim around the tank as she tried to come to grips with her life. Ky'Nasia messed around with a wack ass nigga and ended up with an STD. She just wanted RahKe to see how it felt for someone else to get all her time and attention, but she ended up fucking herself over. She just wanted him to feel and understand the pain she was experiencing.

A few weeks went by and Ky'Nasia was back living with

Ke and his mother. Every day she walked outside she could see Shatek's house. That bothered her bad, but she didn't let it affect her. She went to the doctors and found out she was having a boy. She sent photos of the ultrasound out immediately. Nothing could ruin her day. She was getting her labor induced on November 7th, 2006 at 8 am, then she would have her prince. The world was hers. RahKe called her phone all excited and asked when she would be home. She told him she was about to pull up. RahKe was in front of the house waiting when 'Nasia got home. He kissed her like crazy. They hadn't had any contact since the last issue other than sleeping in bed together whenever Ke came home. Giving him a boy must have made his day. He rubbed her belly and kissed it. "The only thing greater than me is my boy." RahKe screamed that as they walked into the house.

The baby shower was two weeks away and we finally knew the sex of the baby. Ready to get all the baby stuff together, RahKe got everything on the list. He was very happy to be having a boy. Ky'Nasia did all the prep for her baby shower. She had no help, but she handled her business. At the baby shower, Ky'Nasia got hit with a low blow as she hung her 'It's a Boy!' balloons on the step. She looked down the street at Shatek's house to see the same fucking balloon. Tears poured out of her eyes. Not only was she pregnant, but she was having a boy too. They ended up having boys eight days apart. 'Nasia shook her head, "I have NEVER had anything to myself with RahKe." The battle of who would get the name junior was in full effect. She had her baby first, but Ky'Nasia's son was destined to be a junior. It's sad how Ky'Nasia couldn't see the forest for the trees. The disrespect was at an all-time high and her pain was deep.

Ky'Nasia went into labor at 3:47 am on November 7th, 2006. Her prince was born at 6:06 am. He weighed six pounds and seven ounces, and was nineteen and a half inches long. He had a head full of jet black, curly hair. His eyelashes were long, and they curled like a girl's. The doctors ran tests on him to check for the bacteria that was in his intestines. They couldn't find any trace of it. They monitored him closely. They would continue to run tests on him for the first year of his life.

RahKe Quan Jenkins, Jr. was here. RahKe held his son so tight and wouldn't let him go. When the baby cried to eat, RahKe would hold him up to 'Nasia's titty so he could eat. RahKe had the baby glued to his hip the entire time they were in the hospital. RahKe was in love, and it showed.

When she got home, reality smacked her in the face. All of the feelings of hurt and pain returned as she thought about how that nigga had another baby and on the same fucking street. The knife that was once in her back was now jammed in her neck. Her air was slowly being cut off. She tried to focus on the positive like the fact that her baby boy was alive and well. She pushed all the negative thoughts to the side as she regained her ability to push forward. Her kids were her driving force to keep fighting. ZahNyah and RahKe Jr. were her reason for everything. The grind never stopped for them.

Round 10

A Major Hit

Round ten lifted Ky'Nasia off her feet with an uppercut as RahKe got sucked deeper into the street life and the drug game. RahKe was moving fast and reckless. He started doing the unthinkable. He was having parties left and right, and the cops were there every step of the way, watching everything that was going on at the house. 'Nasia was working and taking care of the kids. She urged Ke to leave the streets alone, but the more she tried the harder he went. Ke made sure they had everything they needed. Unfortunately, he was very flashy and could care less who knew what he was into, he was a real hustler and a thug. The women never stopped calling or dropping by either. RahKe was still doing his dirt, just not as much or as open as before.

RahKe was on the front porch barbecuing on the grill. All his boys were there, and they were smoking weed and drinking Hennessy. The music was on full blast. Ky'Nasia came onto the steps just as the DT's pulled up on them. "RahKe, you know we are watching you. Turn the music down and take the grill off the step. It needs to be at least ten feet from the house. By the way, I saw the blunt you tried to kick on the step. Have a nice day." The

DT tipped his hat and got back into his van. RahKe picked up the blunt and lit it when the cops pulled off. He and his boys continued to party on the front step.

Broad street was jumping that summer, and the breeze felt good. Everybody was outside. Ky'Nasia got some money from RahKe to get her and the kids ice cream and her some wine. 'Nasia was a queen and whatever she wanted she got. RahKe did his best to keep her happy. He didn't want to lose her. Ke handed her a fifty dollar bill, "Bring me back a pack of Dutches and a black and mild please. I love you."

"Is the rest mine?"

"Of course. Do you have to ask?" RahKe rolled his eyes because he knew she was going to spend it anyway.

"Nope. I love you too. I want crabs later and this ain't enough." She smiled as she got the kids in the car because she knew he was going to make it happen. After getting home from having ice cream, the kids wanted to go to the park with Nikki. 'Nasia changed the kid's clothes and let them go to the park. It was perfect, now she could drink her wine and have some grown up time. Ky'Nasia pulled her wine out of the freezer and poured her a glass. She sat in the window and watched the people outside. RahKe came into the house and kissed her. "Are you ready to eat? The food is done. You know you have to make our plates before I let them niggas eat. I do this for y'all. For us. Them niggas come last," Ke said as he kissed her forehead and headed to the kitchen. RahKe returned with a stack of paper plates. He handed them to 'Nasia, "Go make plates for the house, so them niggas can eat." RahKe was rubbing his hands across Ky'Nasia's ass. She started to get up as Ke stuck his finger in her pussy, "I think I want some of this. Who told you that you could wear these little ass shorts? Don't be showing anybody my goodies. You're gonna get somebody hurt." He continued to play with her pussy.

"Stop Ke! Let me go make the plates. You know them niggas are waiting to eat. That's their main reason for hanging around – to freeload off of us! They never bring shit to the table, but always got they hand out." Ky'Nasia tried to get off the couch, but RahKe pushed her down. He bent her over the couch, "Ain't nobody asked you about that. I got us. Let me worry about who freeloads off of me." RahKe slid her shorts to the side and inserted his dick in her pussy. "We got to be quick 'cause you know they will be knocking soon." Ke got that pussy going fast. Ky'Nasia was enjoying every moment of it until she heard the door opening. "Get the fuck out," RahKe yelled as his boy Cuff opened the door. Shaking his head, "I'm gonna fuck him up. He knows better than to open my door without knocking, especially when you or my kids are here." RahKe continued to beat that pussy up. 'Nasia's body began to shake. She was nutting all over Ke's dick. He felt the rush of nut and went harder. He bent her over a little more and spread her ass cheeks open. He fucked her rough. He jammed his dick in her for a few more strokes before he busted everywhere. Ke leaned in and kissed the side of her face. "Go clean yourself up and come make plates while I go fuck this nigga up for opening my door." RahKe waited for 'Nasia to get upstairs before he went outside.

Ky'Nasia was in the shower and could hear RahKe cursing Cuff out. "Why the fuck you open my door without knocking? When my wife and kids are home, there is no reason for you to even enter my motherfucking house. That's the fastest way to get your ass beat. I started to beat the shit out of you. You better thank 'Nasia when she comes out for talking me out of fucking you up. You better be lucky she was covered or else." 'Nasia quickly showered and got dressed. She came down and made the plates for the house. Walking back inside she could feel Cuff staring at her, so she turned and looked at him.

"I am sorry for coming in the crib without knocking first. I thought Ke had forgotten about the food. I didn't mean no disrespect," said Cuff. He dropped his head and walked away. In fact, Cuff stayed away for a few days. Knowing how hard Ke had just come down on him, she understood him leaving at that moment. Ky'Nasia put the plates away for later. She grabbed a hotdog roll and headed back to the grill. She picked the prettiest hotdog with the most BBQ sauce. She didn't eat burnt hotdogs. She had a hamburger roll for RahKe because she always made sure her man ate. RahKe slapped her ass as he bit into the burger.

"That's why got Cuff got cursed the fuck out. Now leave my ass alone," she whispered.

"His bitch ass was probably thinking about it when you came out here to make those plates. I'm gonna fuck him up." RahKe couldn't resist as he ran his hands from her ass to her pussy. "I will kill a nigga over this. This is my shit." Ke turned around to address the rest of the niggas on the step. "Hey motherfuckers! Y'all see this beauty Queen right here. If y'all ever try to cross her in anyway, I will kill you. I mean in any way; rolling your eyes, slick talk, trying to get at her, or even thinking about it. You're dead and I put that on everything!" The look in his eyes said it all. The sweat instantly beaded up on his nose. "Please relay the message to Cuff. Nobody is exempt. She is my everything. I will not share this one." He grabbed her and kissed her roughly in the mouth. Ke was drunk, but they knew he meant what he had said.

It was May 25th, 2008 and the weather was nice. RahKe decided to throw a party at Nikki's crib. He bought a bunch of liquor like Hennessy, Absolute, Grey Goose, and Paul Masson. There were chips, pretzels, and hotdogs. Everything was free and the ladies served the drinks. It was so packed in there that they could barely dance. It was lit for it to be a house party. There were even people in the backyard. The music was jumping. Ky'Nasia and Olivia stood in the middle of the party reppin' their hood. "DGP (Delsea Gardens Posse) for life." The niggas in the party started getting hype and yelling their sets and hoods. Ke noticed that niggas were getting mad and had to lay down the law. Nobody was allowed to disrespect Ky'Nasia. The niggas respected it and kept their cool. Ky'Nasia was always going to do what she wanted, and nobody could stop her.

She heard some chicks arguing in the back room. She went to calm down the situation, but this one chick, Destiny, got beside herself. 'Nasia always gave a fair warning before she fucked shit up, so she asked Destiny to leave her alone and mind her damn business. Destiny continued to follow 'Nasia around the party poppin' shit. Destiny loved to talk, and 'Nasia wasn't with that shit. Ky'Nasia couldn't take anymore. She popped the bitch in the mouth, and the fight was on. 'Nasia's nephew, Bo, cleared the house. Ky'Nasia beat that bitch's ass and then Ke, Bo, and Olivia came to help fuck shit up even more. Before she could catch herself, 'Nasia had ripped Destiny's ponytail off her head and threw it outside. It got crazy way too fast. Before the fight was finished the cops were there and started spraying mace on people. They didn't care who they were or what they were trying to do.

RahKe was getting beat up by a cop, so Ky'Nasia had to protect her man. She drew her fist back and punched the cop in the jaw. The officer pulled out his mace and sprayed everyone in the room, then he called for backup. It was an all-out riot on Dock and Board Street! Everybody that was close to RahKe and 'Nasia was there fighting the cops. Ke, Bo, and a few other niggas got locked up that night. Ky'Nasia, doing what she did best, had Ke's back and came up with the money. She bailed him and Bo out of jail that morning. Ke was charged with possession of drugs that night. The next day Ke got his boys out. Board street was hot. The police beat the block down for three days strong after that party. RahKe became more and more reckless instead of slowing down. He had feigns coming to the crib and meeting him in the alleyway. He knew the rules; never hustle out of your own crib, never keep anything in the crib where you rest your head, and never let too many niggas know your next move. All of these things RahKe let slip his mind because he was facing life in prison. He was just caught up and in too deep. They didn't bother him too much after the party because they were building a case against him. They wanted him badly. RahKe did what he wanted, and it showed in the streets.

On July 18th, 2008, RahKe prepared for his birthday block party. He had a box of Dutches, weed, Hennessy, and Heineken. They set up in the living room and rolled in an entire box of Dutches. The party was on his birthday, July 19th and everything was free again. They had real food like crabs, chicken, tuna salad, baked beans, hamburgers, hot dogs, chips, water, and soda. Ky'Nasia was in charge of the blunts. She decided who could get one and how many they could have. RahKe made sure that they knew that whatever 'Nasia said was final. There were niggas from every hood and every set there. They partied and had a good time. For once, it didn't get turned out. Niggas left the party high and drunk. There were so many blunts on the ground that niggas couldn't finish because they were too done. The only reason the cops showed up was to tell them to turn down the music and be safe getting home. The party ended at 1:30 am. RahKe and Ky'Nasia made sure everyone left the area and went home. Once home and ready for bed, they made sure they had everything put away and cleaned up. That night they held each other and made promises to never let anything come between them. RahKe told Ky'Nasia how much he appreciated the way she handled herself at the party. Ke was falling asleep while talking. 'Nasia kissed him goodnight and let him go to sleep.

RahKe and Ky'Nasia had a family day the next morning. RahKe paid for them to go to Wildwood Water Park. Ke didn't swim, so he watched their stuff while everybody else enjoyed the water. He waited for 'Nasia to get out the water to eat. They walked on the boardwalk while the kids stayed in the water with Ke's Mom. Before leaving the boardwalk, Ke bought everybody a treat. The kids wanted funnel cake and ice cream, and of course, they got what they wanted because they were Ke's kids. He didn't mind spending the money because it made them happy. He did anything for them. They headed home after a day filled with family and fun. The kids were passed out and sleeping in the back of the car. RahKe carried them into the house. Ky'Nasia got the kids washed and dressed for bed while Ke handled some last-minute business. 'Nasia showered and made a few sandwiches for her and Ke. She set everything up in the room and waited for Ke to come back. He came back two hours later, but 'Nasia was asleep. Ke hopped in the bed and kissed her goodnight.

Ky'Nasia just so happened to get up to use the bathroom and heard a lot of arguing outside the house. She looked out the window to see RahKe's right-hand man out there. She shook Ke. "Ke get up! Duke is out there arguing and about to fight. They have their guns out and everything. Go get them off this block. Our kids are here."

Ke jumped up to see what she was talking about while throwing on some clothes. "I'm gonna handle it," Ke said as he grabbed the gun out of the closet.

"Be careful. We need you." She kissed him and grabbed a hug before he left. Watching out the window she saw RahKe hit the corner.

"Y'all niggas got a problem? Y'all know this my block and ain't shit jumpin' off on this end."

Big Ace said, "No disrespect big dog, but this ain't got nothing to do with you. This is about the homies and shit."

"Cool and I respect that, but my kids live on this block so ain't no shooting and shit happening here. Y'all gonna have to take that shit somewhere else. Ain't shit like that happening here."

Duke let RahKe know that he was good, but Ke continued to stand there. "I ain't about to argue with no niggas that I know are mad 'cause you took over the block and they can't eat. They wanted me to step to you over some fiend shit, but I handled it."

"They wanted you to check me? Yeah, okay. This is my block! Which one of y'all niggas gonna check me? I run this shit. I make the money 'cause my shit is better! Now, if we got a problem swing. I ain't with no gang shit, but I got a team that will knock your motherfucking dick loose. So, what y'all want to do?" Big Ace and Pop shook RahKe's hand and stepped off. RahKe watched as they hit the corner. He chilled on the block with Duke for about an hour to make sure shit was calm. Ke came in the house, and Ky'Nasia could finally go back to sleep.

The summer was coming to an end and things seemed to be going well until the shit hit the fan. It was August 10th, 2008, and the heat was on. The cops were watching the block from every angle. The bail bondsman came to the house to get RahKe because he had missed his court date. RahKe went with them and they were able to get him a new court date. They gave him a new bail and he had to pay a two-hundred-and fifty-dollar fee. That pissed Ky'Nasia off. RahKe was at court all morning and she had shit to do. He called her to tell her he was home but had to make a run really quick. He said he would be back in less than one hour.

'Nasia was ready to go, so she walked home from Dana's house. She was going to get money to buy cards. She wanted to play Uno, Phase 10, and Rummy.

When she got to the house, Ky'Nasia seasoned her food and put it in the oven for dinner. She made roast beef with carrots and red-skinned potatoes. She set the oven for three hundred because it was early, and she wanted it to slow cook. RahKe walked out the door to meet the weed man and came right back home. Ky'Nasia sat on the chair holding RahKe, Jr as Ke walked in the house with a big ass bag of weed. Before 'Nasia could smell it or Ke could say what it was called, the door was kicked in. There were cops and DT's everywhere. They threw Ke to the ground and put Bo to sleep on the living room floor. They came in from the kitchen asking whose drugs were in the kitchen as they had their guns drawn. They ransacked the house like crazy. They kept everyone in the living room while they searched the perimeter of the house. After they had everybody and the dogs under control, they moved them to the backyard. As they came in the house with dogs and more back up, they continued to raid the house. They poured the sugar and cereal out onto the floor. They treated the house like it was shit. They ripped the clothes out of the closets and dressers and pulled the kid's bedroom apart. They even cut open one of the mattresses. Ky'Nasia was in complete shock. RahKe could only shake his head. Ky'Nasia said nothing because she knew that the shit had officially hit the fan. Ke was going to jail for real. She kept herself together and didn't show the cops any fear. They were trying to destroy them. Since they couldn't get them to talk, they took everybody to the station. The weak ones only confessed to what was theirs. They were charged for their shit and were released. Ky'Nasia, her sister Dana, Bo, and RahKe, on the other hand were all charged with possession of an unlawful weapon, a gun, and received mad drug charges. They were going to jail. Before leaving the station, RahKe told

Ky'Nasia, "I love you and we're gonna be okay." They put them in separate cars to take them to the county jail.

Ky'Nasia and Dana were in the same car. They talked shit to the officers and told them their wives were home sucking and fucking a big black dick while they out playing 'Robocop'. The officers were getting very pissed and upset. After they arrived at the county, the cops pulled them out of the car and slammed them up against the wall. Hungry and tired, Ky'Nasia asked the CO if they had something she could eat. They laughed at her and told her that this wasn't Burger King and she couldn't have it her way. 'Nasia knew things were going to get worse. RahKe's bail was $250,000 again. Ky'Nasia's and Dana's bails were $25,000. The doors slammed behind them.

Ky'Nasia hit the unit in the jail and all the fiends came running. They took good care of her and told her not to worry because Ke was coming. Little did they know he was in the next block over. 'Nasia knew it was only a matter of time before she and her sister were bailed out, so she was chilling. Dana, on the other hand, was wildin'. She cried the entire time. Everybody in there wanted her to shut the fuck up, including Ky'Nasia. Ky'Nasia knew her sister wasn't built for jail.

The next morning DYFS (Division of Youth and Family Services) came to the jail to see them. Ky'Nasia found out they had removed her kids from their grandma's house because the cops said the drugs were in the reach of her children. She damn near lost it. She snapped on the social worker and demanded to be taken back to her cell. Dana didn't have to worry about her child because the father wasn't in her home because he didn't live there. She still cried like a baby at the thought of losing him. Ky'Nasia was fed up with the bullshit. She called RahKe's mom to find out why she let them take her kids, and what was going on. She didn't have any information, so 'Nasia hung up on her. She called her mother to see what was going on with her getting bailed out. She was told to sit tight because someone was coming to get them. They just wanted to get them both at the same time. They had to stay strong.

For the entire three days of incarceration, Ky'Nasia didn't eat or shower. She brushed her teeth and took a birdbath at the sink in the cell. Her cellmates hated her for that, but they couldn't say shit. They knew Ky'Nasia was just as raw and fucked up as they were. On a Thursday night, Dana looked out the window and saw her brothers and other people there to post their bail. Then around 2 am, she saw them get into their cars and leave. She began to cry all over again. That shit was annoying. Ky'Nasia snapped, "Yo! Shut the fuck up! You know we're getting out. It's the middle of the night and we're females. They are not about to let us leave. It would be on them to let us go and something happen to us. Take your stupid ass to bed and we will be out in the morning." Ky'Nasia always had to be strong because Dana was weak.

The next morning, they heard their names called and ran to the door. "Your family came and bailed you guys out last night, but we couldn't let y'all both go until this morning. After breakfast, y'all can roll up."

"We ain't eating that shit! Can we go now," Ky'Nasia asked? She hadn't eaten anything the entire time, except a slice of bread. She was ready to go home to pick up the pieces of her life. She also had to figure out what was going on with her kids. Waiting on them to yell 'roll up,' 'Nasia and Dana watched through the window as the rest of the unit ate breakfast. They popped the door open one hour later, and they got up out of there. RahKe and Bo were still locked up.

It was 6:50 am and they were walking up Board Street in Bridgeton trying to get to a phone or a ride to Millville. They reached Mrs. Joy's house and made a few phone calls and found a ride home. Once Ky'Nasia got home, she had to deal with the press trying to record her house and asking her for statements. She wasn't in the mood for that bullshit, so she cursed them out. They finally got the hint and left. Her house was trashed from top to bottom. She began cleaning up in the kitchen. It stunk because the roast she had cooked the other day was still in the oven and it had spoiled. She got rid of that first. RahKe called the minute he thought she was home. He talked a lot of shit. She just listened and cried because he accused her of telling, not knowing that she hadn't said anything. She started trying to figure out how to get Ke out of jail, but nobody wanted to post bail for him because he was a high risk. RahKe got knocked for selling drugs while out on bail, and then the shit thickened.

Being raided and having the house stripped down was a bit too much for Ky'Nasia. She had two kids and no help. She remembered how Ke had two girls and two boys. Both of the girls were the same age and both of the boys were the same age, and that hurt her to her core all over again. Tears streamed down her face as she tried to figure out how she was going to take care of her kids. RahKe was pressuring her to get him out before his next court date. He wanted to fight his first case from the streets, but it wasn't looking good. Ky'Nasia stopped looking for bail bondsmen and started looking for lawyers to represent RahKe. She had to prepare for the long run. This round was rough and she was trying to get her balance back and remain strong. She had to continue to fight.

Round 11

Ride or Die Footwork

Ky'Nasia was barely breathing in the eleventh-round, as she began her first bid with "Clyde." They put in for countless bail reductions, but the courts decided not to grant him bail. Ky'Nasia was going up to North Jersey with RahKe's side bitch, Shatek, trying to bail him out of jail. 'Dear God, help me,' was all she could say. It took everything in her not to fuck that bitch on the way there and back. What was she doing? All of this for a guy who was still getting visits from his side piece. Ky'Nasia should have known better, but his hold on her life was stronger than she thought.

In March of 2009, Ky'Nasia started nursing school at Lincoln Tech. She was ready to make boss moves for her family. She had to quit her job and collect unemployment because she had to give nursing school her all. She did just that. She was passing all her classes with a B+ or higher. Her baby girl was in school at Child Family Center and her son was with a babysitter. She really didn't care for the babysitter, so she had to make other arrangements. That kind of put a dent in how she moved because no one was reliable. Not even for something as important as school. Halfway through school, she was able to hire a lawyer to represent RahKe on his murder case. He wanted $25,000. Ky'Nasia knew it was worth it to save Ke's life. She gave the man his down payment and sent him his weekly payments to help Ke. School was coming to an end and RahKe's trial for his life had just begun.

On March 20th, 2010, they went to trial. The lawyer did the damn thing! He had the judge stumbling over his own words. He tore the state witnesses apart and had them changing their statements under oath. The dude was nothing, but amazing, and things were looking up for RahKe. As the trial came to an end, it was time to read the verdict. The courtroom was flooded with police and state troopers. RahKe's mom and Ky'Nasia sat in the courtroom holding hands as the jury stood to read the verdict out loud, "Felony murder – not guilty." The room disappeared as the tears of joy streamed down their faces. "Thank you Jesus," was all they could say after every "Not guilty" that left the jury's mouth. The lawyer said it just as loud as Ke's Mom and Ky'Nasia. The family members of the victim said any and everything out of their mouths to RahKe in the courtroom, but the cops were on 'Nasia and Ke's mom. Ky'Nasia whispered to Ke's mom, "I guess we are the threats and not the people who are verbally thrashing RahKe." They both smiled because the hard part was over, and the rest was up to God.

Ky'Nasia graduated nursing school on April 1st, 2010. That was one of the happiest days of her life. She accomplished her goal and had something that she could say she did on her own. Though she still had to prepare for her boards, she was an LPN, and nobody could get the credit for her doing that with two kids, no job, and no help. She went out with her friends and family to celebrate at Applebee's. They toasted and ate good meals. Ky'Nasia was now waiting on Ke's sentencing date for his drug and gun charges and the attempted burglary with a weapon charge. They talked on the phone, and he thanked her for the lawyer and congratulated her on finishing school. He knew there were times she wanted to give up, but quitting wasn't in her. She was grateful that he showed her some type of love and appreciation, so she didn't want to tell him what his boys were saying about him. She continued to do her part.

RahKe's sentencing day was on May 14th, 2010. Ky'Nasia, her kids, Ke's mom, and his sisters were there to show the judge that RahKe had support and a family who cared. The judge spoke harshly to Ke before he even heard the victim's family members speak. After the victim's family poured out their heart to the judge, it was time for sentencing. The judge gave RahKe the maximum amount of time for each charge he had. He tried his best to throw the book at him. He ended up with eleven years and eight months. He would be eligible for parole after doing eighty-five percent of his time. RahKe was shipped off to CRAFT for a health assessment on June 10th, 2010. CRAFT was a hard time for them both because they couldn't talk to each other. All RahKe could do was write letters. Ky'Nasia had a lot going on trying to take care of business out on the streets. She wrote back as best as she could. They were fighting to get Ke sent somewhere close.

By the end of June, RahKe was sent to Yardville, which was way over in Bordentown, NJ. The drive was an hour and forty-five minutes from home. They were both disappointed in the drive and how far away from home RahKe was housed. When Ke's visiting list was finally approved, he called to let Ky'Nasia know when she could start coming to see him. RahKe wanted a visit every weekend. After not seeing RahKe or talking to him for almost two months, Ky'Nasia wanted to see him every weekend too. Hearing Ke's voice for the first time in a while made her heart jump for joy. All he could say was that he loved and missed her.

The first visit was crazy and a shell-shock for Ky'Nasia and the kids. When Ky'Nasia and the kids pulled up to the prison, the line was out to the parking lot. There were police parked at the entrance giving out tickets. They had their dogs there to smell for drugs, something that was very different from the county. They got in line as Ky'Nasia read all the rules for visitations. There were things that they couldn't wear and things that they couldn't do. Reading the rules gave her an instant headache. She quickly looked over what she and the kids had on to make sure her visit wouldn't be denied. After an hour of waiting in line, they were almost in the building when one of the officers walked up to Ky'Nasia and said, "You might want to go get an outfit from Walmart. They might not let you in with that dress on." Trying to figure out why they would turn her away the line moved up, and they were in the building. Ky'Nasia was next in line. The guards searched her and the kids. They were all up in their personal space and saying slick shit under their breath. Ky'Nasia wanted to snap, but she knew she was in their world. She knew that any little thing she did or said would stop her visit, so she sucked it up and dealt with it. The guard let her in but informed her not to wear that dress again.

Finally, in the visit hall, they sat and waited for RahKe to come out. There was nothing for the kids to play with or do while they waited for their visit. RahKe came down with only forty-five minutes left of the visitation hours. They were both upset, but it was their first visit. Neither one of them knew what to expect, so Ky'Nasia took a mental note to be in line early next week. When RahKe came out the doors, the kids ran up to him almost knocking him down. Ke picked them both up and carried them to their seats. RahKe and Ky'Nasia hugged and kissed the minute he was close enough to get her hands on him. The guards let them know that they couldn't kiss a lot and they had to keep it to a minimum, in fact, they could only do it at the beginning and end of their visit, and without tongue. They also couldn't touch all over each other or their visit would be terminated. They just looked at each other and sat down. Ke was so happy to see them. He played with the kids and talked to Ky'Nasia. He explained the things he needed and how much money he needed. 'Nasia took a mental note of all the things he requested. They held hands and talked a little more. Ke had a TV within days of being in prison.

The visit was over, and they hated to see Ke go. It was hard to hold back the tears as RahKe got up and kissed them goodbye. The kids held their dad tight and cried hard. That broke Ke's heart. He hugged them tight and kissed them. He told them he would call them later. Ky'Nasia had to remain strong and comfort her crying babies. "It's okay. Daddy's gonna call y'all later." She squeezed her babies trying to ease their pain. The guards took RahKe back and they had to leave the visit hall. Ky'Nasia felt a piece of her soul leave with Ke. She got in the car and the tears began to fall. How was she going to do that every weekend? She got herself together and prepared for the long ride home. She turned the music up and hit the highway. The kids were asleep halfway through the ride and 'Nasia was left to think about her life and how things were going to go from there on out.

After getting the kids out of the car, they sat at the table while talking about the visit and eating. The kids were mad that they had to leave their dad and that they didn't have anything to play with while they were there. Ky'Nasia tried to explain to them that their dad had to stay there for a while and that would be how they saw him for a minute. The kids didn't understand. They went to get ice cream and waited for RahKe's call. They all cuddled up on the couch and watched movies until they dozed off. RahKe called at about 8:35 pm. He had to get himself together because it broke his heart to see his kids crying for him. Ke didn't want his kids to go through that every week, so he told Ky'Nasia to bring them up there once a month and around the holidays. 'Nasia agreed. She hated seeing her babies hurt for their dad like that. She handed the kids the phone, and they had a list of things to tell him already. They were happy they got to see their dad. This was only the beginning of a seven and a half year bide. That was now their fucking life.

It was Christmas Eve and Ky'Nasia and the kids were at the prison for their visit. They hadn't heard from RahKe in two days. Not wanting to miss the visit, they took the drive anyway. When they got there, there were only a few families in the parking lot talking. No one was in line. Ky'Nasia asked the guards what was going on and if there was visitation that weekend. The guards informed her that visitation hours were canceled due to the prison being on lockdown and that there would be no visitation hours next week either. She also asked when the inmates would be allowed to call home. The guard said, "When the lockdown is lifted, they will be able to use the phones again." She was sick that it was a holiday and she couldn't see or talk to RahKe. She got back in the car and took the kids home. Trying to make up for the hurt on her kid's faces, they baked cookies and made hot cocoa with marshmallows. That was the first holiday they didn't get to see or hear from RahKe. It was super hard on them.

Christmas wasn't the same that year. They opened their gifts in silence. Ky'Nasia made sure she took as many pictures as possible so RahKe wouldn't miss a minute of it. They ended up in bed early because they knew RahKe couldn't call. Ky'Nasia held her babies in her arms trying her best to heal the emptiness in their hearts. They hadn't seen RahKe for two weeks in a row. Ky'Nasia also waited to hear from RahKe. He finally called on January 5th. He let her know that the lockdown was lifted, and he could call and receive visits again.

Ky'Nasia was handling her business like a boss. She worked as an LPN doing home care and facilities while taking care of the kids and RahKe. 'Nasia started feeling alone and had no one to talk to about her issues. Working as a nurse made getting money a little less stressful, but she had no one to hold her at night and treat her like a lady. There was no one to fix her broken pieces. She couldn't talk to RahKe because he was no help and couldn't handle her honesty about wanting to go on dates. Then again, it's not like RahKe did any of that with her while he was home anyway, but it was something she'd always wanted, a real relationship. She felt abandoned until Malachi hit her up one day. She talked with him for a while and then almost every day. She let Malachi know the rules from the start.

Rule #1: RahKe and her kids come first!

Rule #2: Never discuss her and RahKe's business.

Rule #3: Never think it was more than what it was because when RahKe gets out everything goes back to normal.

Malachi agreed to the rules and played his part. They went on dates and spent time together, but Ky'Nasia never let her feelings for RahKe change. He always remained number one in her heart. Malachi knew he could never take RahKe's position, but he did his best to fill his shoes while he was away. The conversation between the two of them was the best. They sat in the car and watched many sunsets together. There was always peace with Malachi. He was her escape, for the time being, and she enjoyed his company and caring nature. Malachi NEVER had Ky'Nasia just for him. She was always RahKe's queen and that was very clear.

For many years later, the weekend visits continued, but the time seemed to be going by in slow motion. When it was time for

RahKe to be transferred to a different prison, he was happy because he was closer to home, and his time was getting shorter. The drive was shorter for Ky'Nasia and that made it a little easier on her. After the transfer was complete, Ke's stuff was stolen, so Ky'Nasia had to put more money on his books. He was able to get his food and the things he needed restocked. 'Nasia continued to bust her ass to make sure RahKe had what he needed. RahKe had everything the week it hit the commissary. He ordered a tablet and a Walkman, so he could listen to music while he worked out. He used the tablet so that he could text 'Nasia and that she could send him pictures herself. It was the type of pictures that couldn't be sent through the mail. He wanted to see what he'd be touching when he finally got home. Ke made a lot of promises in the last few months about how he was going to change and be a better man for Ky'Nasia and the kids. 'Nasia wanted to believe him so bad, but Ke was already lying about letters he was getting from Shatek. RahKe promised to ask for a break before ever cheating on Ky'Nasia again.

The long haul was over, and it was almost time for RahKe to come home. Ky'Nasia knew she had to cut ties with anything and everything that would threaten her relationship with RahKe. She slowly let all her interest in other male attention die, then she let Malachi know that she would no longer be seeing or spending time with him anymore. She told him that RahKe would be home in less than six months and she didn't want anything to interfere with them being a family. She grinded harder than ever as she began to purchase clothes, shoes, and all the things RahKe would need when he touched the streets. She had things in motion before he could even ask. Ky'Nasia took great care of her man.

RahKe was a fast talker. He knew how to make people believe that he was serious about what he said and that he would do exactly what he promised. It made Ky'Nasia hold onto his every word. He never wanted for anything the entire bide but all his promises of being there for her and the kids went down the drain. She worked doubles and triples to make ends meet for them as a unit. RahKe had everything he asked for and more, but the closer it was to his release, the more he needed. Yes, baby girl took great care of "Daddy" while everything else around her fell apart. Ky'Nasia struggled to get a car and get back and forth to work. She struggled with making sure their kids had everything and didn't want for anything. All for Bae! Everybody's hands were in her pockets, except her own. That included RahKe, his mother, her mother, her sister, and their kids. Everyone was good except her. She fought back tears every time Big Brother would say, "I hope he rides for you the way you're riding for him. I would have killed to have a girl hold me down like you do. I am proud of you Sis, but don't get your hopes up thinking things are gonna change just 'cause you were there for him. He's still a nigga. Plus, you got fat! He ain't gonna want no fat girl when he gets out. You better hit the gym."

It was all said in love, but 'Nasia's feelings were hurt because of the possibility of it being true. She knew RahKe was good for stepping out but thought that after she had proved her love by staying, he would stop. She hoped and prayed that it would change. After hearing from Nikki that Shatek was going to visit RahKe and was still talking to him, 'Nasia knew something had to give. She was feeling very weak and slow to come back from the quick jabs to her chin. She was leaning, and it wasn't looking good.

Round 12

A Love TKO

A blow to the ribs sent Ky'Nasia crashing onto the ropes in round twelve. As her opponent began their final "finish her" move, 'Nasia hung on by a thread. On December 29th, 2015, RahKe was released from prison, and everything seemed fine. Ky'Nasia got a hotel room and decorated it with rose petals, balloons, candy, food, and drinks. She had their bags packed and ready to go in the car. She was freshly shaved and headed down the road to get her man. Her excitement was high, and she blasted her music on her way to the prison. She arrived at 7:25 am. She sat in the parking lot for what felt like forever, then RahKe came out at 9:45 am. They kissed and hugged the minute he hit the car. "Get me away from here," he yelled.

After RahKe was released, they pulled over on the side of the road for some quick action. Ky'Nasia had on a short brown sweater dress without panties. She crawled over the seat and onto RahKe's lap. She kissed him passionately. She had missed him so much. Ke ran his hand up her dress. "Damn baby, you really don't have any panties on." He smacked her ass lightly. They continued to kiss as Ke began to play with her nipples. He squeezed her titties as he lifted them to his mouth. RahKe licked around her nipples slowly and flicked his tongue across them. She was dripping wet. 'Nasia ripped his belt open and released Ke's dick from his pants. She stroked it with both hands. As the precum dripped out, she wiped it up with her fingers and sucked it off. Ke jammed her titties into his mouth. "Look at these big ass titties. These have been hiding under those dumb ass T-shirts you were wearing to visit. I miss my pillows and my milk. What happened to my milk?" They both laughed. He sucked on them as if they were his lifeline. Wanting to feel his dick inside her she slid the seat back and laid it out. She turned around and mounted him cowgirl style. His dick entered her slowly. It felt like the deeper it went, the more it swelled. She screamed with joy, and her pussy oozed with juices.

"Damn, 'Nasia. This shit feels good. It gripped my dick so tight. You got me ready to nut right now. Oh, go slow so I can hold on a little longer." Ky'Nasia rode his dick nice and slow. Her pussy was throbbing with every ride. She wanted him to fuck her. She reached down and played with his balls. She couldn't help but enjoy his dick and admire his balls. She released waves of orgasms.

"Baby, I need you to fuck me. I need to feel that you miss and want this pussy. I don't want to be the only one enjoying this moment. Fuck me please. Hit it from the back." A car rode by as they changed positions. RahKe entered her from behind and she melted under him. He started his strokes off slow and gentle. His body was shining with sweat as he picked up the pace. He fucked her rough from the back. RahKe slid his finger across her asshole. That sent shockwaves to her brain and she moaned loudly. "Shit. That feels good." RahKe gripped her ass and thrust forward faster, and as the windows began to fog up, 'Nasia yelled, "Take this pussy, Daddy."

RahKe placed his leg on the cup holder in the middle of the car. He grabbed her waist and fucked her fast and hard. “Give me this pussy. This shit is soaking wet. You hear it talking to me?”

“It's yours Daddy. Fuck me! It’s so deep.”

“Tell Daddy you want this dick. I miss this pussy.” RahKe reached his hand around and played with her clit. Ky’Nasia threw her ass back at Ke. She could hear her juices splashing everywhere. Rahke held on as he gave it right back. He was about to nut. His dick swelled to three times its size and was ripping her walls.

“Baby please! It’s too deep. Slow down.”

“I want it. I need this pussy.” RahKe fucked her without mercy. Her body began to shake as RahKe released a nut so strong it almost knocked ‘Nasia through the seat. They quickly got themselves together. The cars were riding by again slowly. The next time, a guy rolled down the window to make sure they were okay. They drove off and headed to the hotel. They stopped by the store and grabbed a few things so that he could shower and brush his teeth. Once at the hotel, RahKe walked into the decorated room filled with balloons, cake, and drinks. They enjoyed each other for one night, in peace, until the kids realized that their dad was home. They tried to hide it from the kids, but they knew everything. They wanted to see their dad, so the next morning RahKe and Ky’Nasia headed to the house to see the kids. They made a welcome home sign for their dad and bought him the chips and candy that he liked. The kids were excited that their dad was home. They enjoyed their dad and played games with him until Ke was ready to go back to the hotel room. Ke only wanted certain people to know he was home, but on the way to the hotel, they made a few stops. At the hotel, they continued to spend quality time with each other. They never made it to the movies because being in each other's arms was more important. They headed home to begin their lives together again on December 31st, 2015.

The whispering started a few months later. It went from him hanging out with the boys, to hanging with his baby mama and bae, Shatek; to texts on his phone, and locks on the trap line a.k.a bae line. Ky'Nasia was bae, but so was Shatek. He said his 'I love you's' to both of them. RahKe was back on his bullshit, and the thought of it sent Ky'Nasia into shock. He was in full hoe mode, and there was no stopping him. On April 10th, 2016, Ky'Nasia was in Larry's Bar having a drink, when Dana told her, "Kelly just saw Ke in A.C. with Shatek." That blow to her head made her mind spin!

Ky'Nasia called RahKe to see where he was, but he didn't pick up the phone, so she finished having a few more drinks with Dana. Before leaving the bar, 'Nasia called Ke again. That time, he answered the phone and got smart with Ky'Nasia, then hung up on her, and that was the first red flag. She headed home because she had to work in the morning, and it was already late. She showered and got ready for bed. RahKe was nowhere in sight, and it was 2:55 am. She got in bed and was fast asleep before 3:15 am. The alarm rang out in her ear, it was time for work. She showered and dressed within twenty minutes. Heading out the door, she gave her kids instructions on what to do and eat that day, then she went to work. RahKe never came home that night or that morning. Her heart was broken. She couldn't believe he had done that to her. By the time Ky'Nasia got home, RahKe was sitting on the step. She walked past as if he didn't exist. RahKe tried to blame 'Nasia for him staying out all night. He said, "I don't have a key to get in the house, and I knew you were mad at me. I thought you were gonna make me sit outside."

"Thinking was never your strong suit, now was it? I don't have time for this. I am talking about the fact that you were in A.C. with Shatek, but every time I ask you to go somewhere with me, you're too busy. Now I see you're busy doing Shatek." Ky'Nasia headed to the shower and back to her room. The kids were listening. They were trying to calm their mom down, but they didn't understand why she was crying and hurt. Ky'Nasia cooked dinner and watched movies with the kids. RahKe was gone again. He wasn't even home for three hours! She didn't bother to argue because it wasn't worth it at that moment. She wanted to believe that things were going to be different that time around, so they continued to live life as if it never happened.

Ky'Nasia was a sucker for RahKe, and so, the body blows kept coming. She bought him a motorcycle on April 25th, 2016. He was only supposed to ride on good days; the days with no rain, clouds, or wet roads and make it home before dark. RahKe never liked to listen to or tell the truth. Ke didn't have the bike for a month and already he was breaking the rules. He would ride to Millville until late at night.

On May 2nd, 2016, the weather was starting to get warm. The sun was shining, and the sky was clear. Ky'Nasia called Ke because she wanted him to come and have dinner with them as a family. Ke promised to be home before dark, but 'Nasia could tell he was lying. After the sun began to go down, 'Nasia and the kids had dinner without RahKe. It was getting late and it began to lightly rain. Ky'Nasia got the kids ready for bed and straight for school the next day. It was 8:27 pm when D-rock called her phone, "Ke just fell off his bike. He's hurt pretty bad. The ambulance is on the way to get him. Meet him at the Vineland ER." The phone went dead.

"What? Wait, what did you say?" Ky'Nasia called back as

she quickly threw on clothes to head to the hospital. A million thoughts were running through her mind as she told her kids and Dana that she would be back. She finally got through to D-rock. "Yo, where is Ke? Is he ok? How bad is it?"

"He is awake and talking, but he can't walk. I think he broke something in his legs. He's in the ambulance now. They are taking him to the Vineland hospital. I am about to drop my kids off home and then meet you there. He asked me to come there."

"Ok. I am headed to the hospital now. Does he have his phone? He's calling me now. I will call you back." She clicked over to talk to RahKe. "What happened to you? Are you okay? Did you hit someone or just fell off?" Ky'Nasia was a nervous wreck. She pulled into the hospital and got herself together before getting out of the car. Once in the hospital, she saw the EMT's bringing in RahKe. He was screaming every time they hit a bump. Ky'Nasia rushed to be by his side. She held his hand as they rushed him back to a room. As the doctors flooded into the room, they questioned how fast they could get him to Cooper Hospital to the trauma unit. They did an X-ray and saw that RahKe's pelvis was broken in two places. They were afraid he was going to bleed out if he was moved without stabilizing his hips. They quickly sedated Ke, positioned, and strapped his hips together. RahKe was in so much pain, and there was nothing 'Nasia could do to help him. They decided to transport him to Cooper via ambulance because of the weather. 'Nasia followed the ambulance to Cooper.

RahKe had emergency surgery at 5 am. He was still on a breathing machine when he woke up in the recovery room at 9:24 am. He had rods placed on the outside of his body to hold his hips together. A second surgery was scheduled for May 9th, 2016. Ke laid in bed trying to pull the tube out of his throat. Ky'Nasia was there every step of the way. She was in the final term of her BSN program, but she refused to leave RahKe's side although her finals were in one week. She brought her books to the hospital to study, but it was hard to study with RahKe in so much pain. She catered to his every need. While RahKe was out getting an X-ray, Shatek called his phone several times. Ky'Nasia picked up the phone, "Hello."

"Where is Ke? He told me he would let me know when I could come to see him. I was planning on coming up there today."

"So y'all still dealing with each other?"

"You have to ask Ke. We're doing our thing. He wants to be with me. He tells me he loves me every day. He's just with you 'cause of the kids."

"Well, I will let him know you called." Ky'Nasia hung up the phone as the tears began to fall. RahKe was pushed back into the room and he noticed the tears dropping from her face. He noticed the phone was in her hand and she was reading the messages.

"'Nasia, give me my phone."

"Oh, you want the phone, huh? Do you want to know what your bae, Shatek, just told me or do you just want your phone?"

"I am hurt 'Nasia. She called to check on me. That's it."

"Bye RahKe. Since you are still in the lying business, I am gonna let you and Shatek be great."

"Please don't do this to me right now. I never thought you were the type to kick a guy while he is down. Please don't leave me like this."

Ky'Nasia sat in the room in silence. She watched as the doctors came and checked RahKe's wounds and pain levels. She didn't bother to listen because she was over it all. After all that she had done and been through, there was still more she had to endure. Her breathing became shallow as the feeling of wind being knocked out of her consumed her body. The doctor let her know that he needed to get a blood transfusion and had to push back his second surgery to May 10th, 2016, due to some complications. She listened and translated everything to Ke and his mother. Whenever things were going bad, Ky'Nasia was always right there. She left, and of course, Ke called Shatek. He said he told her it was over, but 'Nasia couldn't believe him.

Everything went well after the second surgery and it was time for recovery. Ke came home and things slowly returned to normal. Ky'Nasia nursed him back to health just to have RahKe skip out on more family outings to be with Shatek. 'Nasia couldn't take it anymore. She tried everything to get RahKe's attention. She rented a car for his birthday, but he used the car to spend his days with Shatek and his boys. Then, Ky'Nasia got a room in A.C. and ordered RahKe some clothes. RahKe came to the room on the night before his birthday and 'Nasia noticed a hickey on his neck. He tried to say she put it there, but she knew better. They hadn't had sex in a week. She held back her tears. They woke up together on his birthday, July 21st, 2016. Ke spent the morning with 'Nasia and the kids, and with a hickey on his neck. They went to breakfast at IHOP and 'Nasia just tried to make the best out of the day.

They all went home to get dinner ready for later. Ky'Nasia stopped to grab a cake and buy RahKe a fitted to match his clothes. When she reached the house, RahKe was showered and ready to go. They discussed plans to have dinner at 5 pm and cut the cake then. RahKe wanted to go hit the streets, so they gave him his gifts. RahKe was happy about his gifts, so much so he went into the room and changed his entire outfit. He kissed them goodbye and said, "See you at 5 pm. I love you." He walked out the door at 12:55 pm. 'Nasia hit the kitchen. She cooked beef BBQ ribs, candied yams, baked mac and cheese, and cornbread. The table was set with candles and wine glasses. The cake was out, and the candles were on it.

Ky'Nasia was fresh out of the shower and her hair was slayed. She called RahKe to see where he was because it was almost six o'clock now. "Ke, what time are you coming? The dinner is ready, and the plates are made."

"I will be there in twenty minutes. I am headed there now."

"Okay. I love you and see you when you get here."

"Alright."

RahKe didn't show up. The kids were getting impatient, so they ate dinner without the birthday boy. Ky'Nasia was hurt. It was his first birthday on the streets, and he didn't care to spend it with her and the kids. She cleaned the kitchen and put the food away as tears streamed down her face. At 11:30 pm, RahKe hadn't called or came home yet. Ky'Nasia called him one more time before heading to bed, but he didn't pick up. She crawled into bed and held her pillow and phone tight in hopes that RahKe would come home or at least call to say he was okay. She tossed and turned all night. She didn't rest well when RahKe wasn't home.

In the morning, the cake was still in the same position from the day before. The kids could see the hurt in their mother's eyes as she cleared the cake from the table. The kids said, "We can still cut it today when Dad comes home. It's never too late to eat cake. He will be here soon." She kissed her kids and continued to clean the rest of the house. They went to the mall and then to the laundromat. She put the clothes away and got the kids some dinner. She finally put RahKe's plate in the fridge. She made sure her house was spotless before showering and heading to bed for work. The kids called their dad before they shut their eyes, but he didn't answer.

It was 4:26 am, and Ky'Nasia's phone started buzzing. It was a text message from RahKe. *"I love you. WYD?"*

"I am glad you're okay. WYA?"

"I will be home soon. I was fucked up."

"Okay. I guess I will talk to you later."

Ky'Nasia didn't know it wasn't RahKe texting her. Shatek played on 'Nasia's phone like she was Ke for hours until 'Nasia started asking questions that only he could answer. Then Shatek admitted that it was her and that RahKe was passed out and sleeping in her bed. Oh, she didn't hold out the fact that they had fucked all day that day. Wow! 'Nasia endured more gut blows as she was told how much Shatek loved him and that he told her he would never stop fucking with her. She quickly dismissed the rest of the conversation because RahKe was waking up and would kill her if he knew she was texting 'Nasia from his phone.

Ky'Nasia went to work with a heavy heart. She wasn't herself after that episode. She took care of her patients and then her phone started to ring. It was RahKe. She stepped outside to take the call. "Hello, RahKe. I am not interested in being in a relationship with you anymore. You can move in with Shatek. I am done." She hung up the phone and continued to do her work. The patient's mother tapped her on the shoulder and pointed to RahKe parked in front of her house. She pretended like she didn't see him. She was told by the patient's mother to go home and take care of business. Ky'Nasia went outside to listen to RahKe's lies.

"I fucked up, 'Nasia. I did some dumb shit. I promise I didn't mean to hurt you. I had every intention on coming home. I don't know why I can't get my shit together. I don't want her. I want you."

"Ke, I love you, but it's over. We have been doing the same bullshit for sixteen years. It's getting old. I don't want to share. It must be real 'cause you stayed with her your entire birthday weekend. It's Sunday Ke! You left on Friday! Talk about a slap in the face. I refuse to be your second option."

"You know that's not true. You and my kids mean everything to me. I won't make it without y'all. Please hear me out. Can we talk when you get off work?"

"Ke, this is stupid. I begged you to go take a break when you got home. Fuck any and everything walking so you could get it out of your system and be faithful to me. You turned it down, talking about you were ready, that it was us against the world, but yet you're back on your bullshit. I will see you when I get off if you care to be around."

Once at home, Ky'Nasia fell victim to the 'I love you's' and 'I never had a good example as to what a real man is supposed to do when he has a good woman' bullshit. She forgave him and took him back. They went on with life as usual, except 'Nasia was badly bruised and swollen. It all seemed unreal until the months passed and the pattern continued. Not only was RahKe fucking Shatek, but he skipped out on dates with Ky'Nasia to be with her. They were supposed to go to her co-worker's wedding, but she was all alone at the wedding while RahKe recorded his side bitch Shatek twerking in lingerie. 'Nasia couldn't breathe. She was up against the ropes fighting with everything she had. Ky'Nasia couldn't get in touch with RahKe, so she went looking for him. She pulled up in front of Shatek's house and saw that her own truck was parked there despite RahKe's text saying, *"I am down bottom at Domo's house."*

Ky'Nasia bones were slowly being crushed with each blow and it caused her to fall over. Her heart was barely beating as the bell rang out, round twelve was over. As she laid motionless on the floor of the ring, they assisted her to her corner where she collapsed again.

She listened to the same old broken record one more time for the sake of love, family, and never giving up on what she wanted. She wasn't a quitter. All of that hell just to end up back at square one. Blood, sweat, and tears were running from her body. She couldn't stop the pain, so she tried to alleviate it by expressing herself to RahKe. He pushed her away, but she tried again. He told her to do her, and her heart stopped as RahKe exited the ring. At that very minute, life as she knew it, ended. Ky'Nasia had made it to the end of the fight, but her body and mind were badly beaten and damaged. She hung on by a single thread and was literally almost dead, but she had made it. Completing twelve rounds with little to no life left, she proved that she was a fighter.

Ky'Nasia picked up the phone to text Malachi, not because she wanted him, but because she needed a man's opinion. He was always one hundred. Malachi told her the shit she didn't want to hear, and Ky'Nasia understood it all. She had opened the window and RahKe kicked in the door. 'Nasia never set rules for Ke to follow. She never left after the first sign of danger. She continued to look for the best in Ke, but always got what was left over. She fought hard to hold a position that was never hers to begin with. She accepted all of the facts and was put on life support as she lost her will to go on.

Chapter 13
A Strong Recovery

Ky'Nasia's brain was swollen, eyes glued shut, her heart was in a million pieces, and her body was limp. She laid there begging someone, "Pull the plug and put me out of my misery!" Flashbacks of events and memories flooded her mind. It was ironic; she had never seen any promise come to pass except the night they took the kids to Funplex. 'Nasia could hear everyone around her saying, "If only she was strong enough to let go," "If only he would have loved her," and "If only she knew she was much better than that; if only someone took the time to tell her." The machines were beeping all around her. Her brain was searching for answers to so many questions. She didn't even know why she wanted the answers to some of these questions because RahKe was never going to change. It was hard fighting twelve rounds doing two rounds at a time. There was no one on her side to tag team with to lighten the blows. There was no one there to switch with to allow her to rest. She realized that she was too weak to recover quickly. She had thought that she could stay on life support and bounce back because she had always gotten up, but reality hit her again. The fight was over, and RahKe had finally won – life had finally won the match. Ky'Nasia reached over and pulled the plug. She left the battle wounded and scarred, but alive.

'Nasia began to realize that there was more to life than just RahKe. She had something else to fight for, and it was worth fighting for. She wiggled one toe at a time as she determined to fight for her life, the life that RahKe so brutally stole and destroyed with his lies, deceit, and wickedness. RahKe destroyed her sanity and turned her into a heartless monster, but even the world was shocked that she was still hanging in there.

Ky'Nasia's breaths were slow and shallow as she called out to God for help. He was the only one who could heal her now. Broken, she made her declaration to God first, and then to RahKe, "I will never give a man so much power and control over me again. I am finished with toxic relationships. I wish you the best of luck in all that you do and touch. My love for you will never die, but in order for me to live, I have to pull the plug and move on. Thanks for the lessons you have taught me, but I must separate myself."

RahKe watched as she laid there helpless. Their kids were holding her hands. He tried to make an excuse as to why it had to happen that way and what 'Nasia did to make him do the things he did. Ky'Nasia blocked him out because she knew he was going to continue to blame her. She grew strength from her kids being in the room. In reality, RahKe was never going to be anything different, and letting go was her only option to heal.

The road to recovery wasn't easy but well worth it. Ky'Nasia began to focus on herself and her kids. She took it one day at a time. Some days were better than others, but the sheer sight or mention of RahKe sent pain straight down her spine. Although she was able to breathe without difficulties, walking on her own was still a struggle. The nightmares were unbelievably insane. She continued to pick up the pieces of her life and build a life centered on God, herself, and her children. After some time had passed, RahKe was finally able to come around and be part of the family events.

Ky'Nasia showed RahKe that there was life after him. He knew he had lost a good woman and that his apologies were never enough. 'Nasia and her kids no longer had to miss out on doing the things that made them happy. They went on trips and traveled because that's what life was about to them, making memories with the ones they loved. RahKe realized what was important, but it was a little too late at that point. Ky'Nasia wasn't willing to go back down that road again.

RahKe began to move and do things differently. He always made sure that 'Nasia's and the kid's needs were met before he did anything for himself or anyone else. He made the effort to put in the time to show 'Nasia that he wanted his family, but she still kept a wall between them. RahKe told her, "I am here and willing to put in the work to get my family back. I was stupid and I took y'all for granted. I never thought you would get sick of my bullshit. I just knew you could handle it all. I never listened or paid attention to what you were saying until it was too far gone. I am very sorry, and if we can't get back to us, can we at least be friends? I pushed you to the limit and now I have to settle for whatever type of connection I can get. I love you."

"Ke, I am nowhere near ready to be friends with you again. Maybe someday I will be able to start our friendship over, but right now I don't think that is wise on my part. I am still wounded and hurt by all of your actions. Honestly, I don't think I could ever trust you again. I don't want to give you false hope. I want to be as far away from you as possible, but for the kid's sake, we will continue to co-parent. I love you, but now, I love me more." Ky'Nasia shook her head as RahKe tried to lean in for a hug and a kiss. He understood and stepped back. 'Nasia was finally able to smile again.

Ky'Nasia took the necessary steps for her to be whole again. She invited RahKe to dinner and they went to the restaurant where it all started, Red Lobster. He opened the door for 'Nasia and they sat down and had a drink while they waited for the food to come out. 'Nasia started the conversation, "RahKe, I invited you here so we could talk without the kids. I want you to know and understand how I truly feel. I forgive you. I've learned a lot from our past and I am trying my best not to let it affect my future. I see your efforts to right your wrongs and it doesn't go unnoticed. Even though you do it, I know that at any given moment you can go right back to the old you. We have been down that road plenty of times. I appreciate the changes you have made and are willing to make. I also wanted to say that I am sorry for the parts that I played in the relationship that caused you pain and to not be able to trust me. I wasn't insane in the matter either. My actions were a reaction to yours, but they were still wrong. I hope you can find it in your heart to forgive me as well."

"'Nasia, I know it was my fault. I didn't have a real example of what a real man should have been. I followed the trend that I saw, and it cost me something that meant the world to me. I forgave you a long time ago. I was just waiting to hear you say you forgave me. I love you and I will not stop making an effort or putting in the time to show you that I really want to be with you and the kids. I have changed and I am glad you see it. I appreciate you allowing me to be in the kid's life and around y'all. Thank you for being able to sit down and talk with me. I have been dealing with my broken areas and I called out to God for help. He is the ultimate healer and deliverer. My relationship with him is stronger now and he is helping me through this. I pray daily for growth and that he heals the hearts of the people I have hurt. I also pray that he helps me to be able to admit to my mistakes and learn from them. I want to be a better man for myself and for my family. Until God is done healing and changing us, I am glad to be a part of the family in the small ways. I will continue to work on myself. Thank you for taking the time out to let me know you noticed the change. I won't go backward. I can't afford to lose you anymore. I love you."

They ordered another round of drinks, and the food hit the table as they continued to talk and reminisce. They laughed at the funny and good memories they had together. They enjoyed each other's company without bringing up the old hurt. Ky'Nasia felt good to be able to be at peace for once. The food was great and they shared a dessert as they hashed out a few deals about the kids that needed to be discussed. They finished up there with everything ending on a positive note. Then, they shook hands. That was the beginning of a new friendship. They took it one minute at a time as they allowed God to mend and heal their wounds.

ABOUT THE AUTHOR

Octavia Adams, Millville, NJ resident and dedicated mother of two, works as a pediatric nurse. When she's not helping with homework and saving little lives, she enjoys writing, shopping, and traveling. Her passion for mentoring and advocating for teenage girls gave birth to her non-profit organization, "Uniqueness on the Rise." She uses this platform to educate young ladies on financial literacy, hygiene, college readiness, and a plethora of other topics.

A graduate of Neumann University, Octavia plans to further her education in the field of nursing while continuing to write a series of books along the way. She believes she's found her niche in writings that inspire the reader to be honest about the places they've been and look forward to what the journey has to offer.

Made in the USA
Middletown, DE
15 August 2020

15302595R00102